GW00739220

DESIRE

The Seductors Series

B.L.WILDE

Copyright © 2013 B.L.WILDE

All rights reserved

The characters and events portrayed in this book are fictitious. Any similarity to real persons, living or dead, is coincidental and not intended by the author.

No part of this book may be reproduced, or stored in a retrieval system, or transmitted in any form or by any means, electronic, mechanical, photocopying, recording, or otherwise, without express written permission of the publisher.

ISBN-13: 978-1493761005
ISBN-10:1493761005

Cover Design Copyright: B.L.Wilde
Cover image: Denis Ivanov43

For my smut loving bitches!

CONTENTS

Acknowledgements

My heartfelt thanks have to go to Jo Matthews first. You are a part of this series as much as me. From the cover design to the editing and the formatting, I couldn't have done this without you. I can't wait for the bright future that is ahead of us. We make quite a team my dear. I love the bones of you woman!

My thanks go out to my pre readers and dear friends Liz and NeeNee. I adore you girls. You give me so much strength in this crazy world of publishing.

Mandy, thank you for helping with the final read thru and catching those little things we missed.

Lastly, thank you to my readers. I hope you enjoy the journey you're about to start.

THE SEDUCTORS SERIES

DESIRE

B.L.WILDE

PROLOGUE

Sex—it can get you anything.

I should know; it's paid my way for the last five years, and I'm not talking about the average wage with the ordinary office job. That would never work for me.

I'm talking about the big bucks—the money that can buy you your dream car and that once-in-a-lifetime vacation you always wanted to take. For me, though, I could have those things every year.

I work for a secret organization called *The Seductors* that specializes in gaining certain objects or pieces of information for our clients. Of course, to seduce a target, you only need one thing: *sex.*

My name is Jade. I'm a *Seductor,* and I can't even explain to you how much I *love* my job.

CHAPTER ONE

"Jade, can you hear me?" I moved slightly, touching my hidden earpiece as I tried to drown out the noise of the room. "I can't open the safe," Zara stressed.

I turned my back to the crowd so no one would see me speak. "What do you mean? You double checked the code, right?" I hated new recruits. This job wasn't something you could just start doing. It came from experience and using common sense. Zara still had a lot to learn.

"Yes. Oh, shit, Jade! Someone is coming!"

"Stay out of view. I'll be there as soon as I can." I turned again, making my way up the grand staircase.

"I'm sorry, Miss. That area is off limits to guests. The party is this way," I heard one of the security men call from behind me.

"Oh, I'm sorry." I acted flustered, turning around and dropping my purse. "I was looking for the restroom." I made sure my left leg was visible through the slit in my red dress as he bent down to pick up my handbag. "I have a run in my stockings and I need to take them off."

"Mmm, is that so?" he mused, still looking at my legs. "I can let you use the restrooms upstairs on one condition." With a smirk on his face, he stood up and handed me my purse. "I'd have to escort you."

"You wouldn't mind?"

"It would be my pleasure," he smoldered, showing me the way upstairs. "Are you here alone?"

"No, I'm here with a friend but I somehow managed to lose her." I smiled shyly, following him as I tried to ignore Zara panicking in my ear piece.

"Jade, someone is right outside!" She needed to shut up before she was overheard and our mission was blown.

"Are you and your friend members of the press?"

"No. Mr. Casey is an acquaintance of ours. "

"Oh, I've heard he has *a lot* of those," the guard chuckled, showing me the door to the restroom. "I'll wait here to escort you back to the party."

This was Zara's first mission; I was only here for backup in case she got into trouble. All new recruits had support on their first few missions. My first assignment had been a similar job to this. Stealing an object from a safe was probably the easiest task to have once you knew the location.

"Jade!" Zara hissed in my ear. "Where are you?"

"I'm in the restroom. Give me a second to stun the guard." I opened the door, leaning seductively against the frame. "I was wondering if you'd give me a hand with my stockings," I purred, watching the guy swallow hard as he eyed me from head to toe.

"I was hoping you'd say that," he smoldered, pushing me inside. I had several amazing gadgets thanks to my line of work. A purse with a built-in stun gun was one of many. I turned my purse to stun as he pinned me against the wall and began to kiss down my neck. "You are so sexy," he groaned, moving his hands down my neck toward my breasts.

"And you're an idiot," I grinned before stunning him just

below his ear. He fell to the ground like a sack of potatoes and I had to laugh. Sometimes they made it too easy.

When I was sure the guard was out cold, I raced down the corridor. Zara and I would only have ten minutes at the most until he woke up.

"Zara, it's clear," I whispered, scanning the hallway.

"I'm sorry," she whimpered, coming into sight. Her brown eyes looked defeated. "Maybe I'm not ready."

"This is your first mission. I won't let you fail, Zara. You can do this! Now, let's get those photos and get the hell out of here!" I winked, grabbing her hand.

Our client was being blackmailed with some racy pictures that had been taken a few years ago. We'd been assigned to get them—along with the negatives—back.

"My hands are shaking," she muttered, running them through her blonde hair.

"Just breathe. We'll be out of here in a matter of minutes."

"I never imagined it would be this intense. Training didn't prepare me for this."

"It comes with experience—trust me," I whispered, making my way over to the safe. "Do you have the code memorized?"

"Yes. Two, four, six, nine, zero." She frowned before adding, "Or was it zero, nine?"

"I'll just use the decoder," I sighed, rolling my eyes. *Recruits!* "We don't have much time left. Watch the hallway while I do this." Within minutes, I had the photos and negatives in my hand.

"Jade, someone is coming!" Zara hissed, rushing over to me. "I think they're onto us." *Great!* Why did I accept this damn mission again? Molly had offered to do it, and now I wished I had let her.

Zara was right, though; I could hear several bodies moving around just on the other side of the door. They must have found the guy in the restroom.

I looked out toward the balcony, knowing it was our only escape route now. I just hoped Zara wasn't scared of heights.

"We'll need to make a quick exit. How are your climbing skills?" I motioned toward the large window.

"I'll race you," Zara giggled, quickly grabbing a head start. Maybe she would fit into the Seductors, after all.

❊ ❊ ❊

"How did it go with Zara?" Miss S.—Sonia to her close friends—asked when I returned to headquarters the next day.

"Really good. She's fearless. She climbed down a building in four inch heels without even batting an eye," I chuckled.

"She sounds like you when you first started," Sonia snorted. "So you think she's ready to go solo?"

"I'd have her do one more mission with a backup just to be safe. She froze a little at the beginning."

"Okay, I'll see who's free. "

"I don't mind watching her again."

"You'll be busy," Sonia smirked.

"You didn't summon me here just for feedback on Zara?" I'd been hoping Sonia had a new mission for me, and it looked like I was in luck. My latest solo mission was almost complete, and I liked to keep myself busy.

"I have a priority mission I want you to take, Jade. The rewards for this one are *huge*," she explained as she passed the paperwork over to me. "It's going to take a few months of hard work to infiltrate the actual home of Mr. Kirkham. As you can see, he owns quite a few properties, but only one of the locations houses the main hard drive that our client needs. I'm sure you can use your talents as an advantage to find out which one, though." I laughed, knowing exactly what Sonia meant. I was one of her top *Seductors*, after all. In the last five years, I had made over fifty million dollars for the company. My looks helped...a lot. I was your typical perfect blonde with clear blue eyes and legs that went on forever. Men fell for my innocent act, but I was *no* angel in real life. It never took a target long to find that out, either. Especially if I chose to take them to bed to gain access to what I'd been assigned to steal. I didn't always *need* to go the whole way, though—I was just *that* good.

Sonia was the *top dog* at the Seductors, and she reported straight to the owner of the organization. I guess you could describe our headquarters in Florida a little like the playboy mansion, except we had guys here, too, and all of us were trained to defend ourselves if we needed to. Rule #6: *Seductors must make sure they are always able to protect themselves from any sudden danger. A monthly refresher is mandatory to renew certification.*

I could only speculate that our founder must have once been a secret agent or in the FBI in the past, because the contacts this organization had could rival that of the Secret Service. I was still trying to work out if that person was a male or female, but either way, our founder was a genius.

As I sat in front of Sonia, I began to look closely over the paperwork. My new target was a Mr. Oliver Kirkham of Kirkham

Industries. He wasn't a bad looking guy according to the picture in his file: tall, dark and handsome—just the way I liked them. His income stats weren't too bad, either. Half a billion dollars in net profits last year. *Damn, that was a lot of money.* He had no partner at the moment, although he had been linked to quite a few women over the last few years. Nothing appeared too serious, however, which was interesting.

It seemed I'd need to travel a bit to track this Mr. Kirkham down. London and New York seemed to be popular places for him.

"When do I leave?" I asked Sonia while I was still reading Mr. Kirkham's file.

"He's due in London next weekend to head up an industrial conference."

"Now, *that* sounds like fun," I teased.

"I'm sure you'll be able to liven up his visit, Jade," Sonia winked. "Make sure you read that file carefully. We have a lot of money riding on this contract, so we can't afford any mistakes."

"Have I ever let you down?" I pointed out.

"Why do you think I've put *you* on this assignment? When do you think you'll complete the job you're on right now?"

"I'll have the diamonds by tomorrow evening," I smirked.

"That quickly?" Sonia looked impressed, but then I had only been on the job for two weeks.

"It's an easy steal. I made first contact yesterday, and of course we hit it off. I'm meeting him at his house tomorrow," I replied.

"You're ruthless, Jade," Sonia grinned before dismissing me.

As I continued to study my new file, it became clear that

Mr. Kirkham was big in the weapons industry. Our client wanted the blueprints for a new machine—the S1030—that was being designed by his company. No wonder this was such a big payout for us.

I had no conscience when it came to stealing, nor did I care who wanted these blueprints. Clients had the choice of remaining anonymous to the chosen Seductor—as was the case with this job—but I never thought about the outcome anyway. This was business. It was all about the money, and this deal was worth five million dollars. It was the biggest mission I'd ever been assigned to, and I *would* succeed. There was no doubt in my mind.

It would be really nice to work on just one case for a few months without having to worry about other assignments; sometimes I felt like a prostitute when I was tasked with seducing more than one target at the same time. This *Oliver* was becoming more pleasing to the eye each time I gazed at him.

Oh, this could even be fun!

"Hey, Sweet Pea. How did it go with Zara?" Molly beamed while I was lying on my bed. She was one of my roomies here at headquarters and a perfect petite brunette. Georgie—my other roommate—Molly and I were often referred to as the three musketeers because, when we weren't on a mission, we were always together.

"Good. She completed it."

"Awesome! What are you reading?"

"Information about my new target."

"Oh, can I see?" she questioned. I had to roll my eyes at her request; she knew the rules. You couldn't go looking into another Seductor's cases. *Rule #3: Case files are confidential. Anyone found sharing information will be dealt with accordingly.*

Everyone knew the '*dealt with accordingly*' part couldn't be good, so no one had broken the rule while I'd been here to actually find out.

A Seductor's contract spanned for ten years. We were tied to those contracts, and if we ran, we would be tracked down and killed. This, of course, was all explained before we signed on the dotted line. It may have sounded horrific—being killed if you ran—but it wasn't. No one would run from this job because the money and perks were limitless. I'd only ever heard of one case, years ago, where it had ended that way, and it was the Seductor's own fault; he didn't obey the number one rule. *Rule #1: Seductors must **never** get attached to their target. If this happens, the mission will be classified as a Code 1 and any further contact between the target and Seductor will be terminated.*

I was halfway through my contract and never wanted it to end.

"Don't you have your own target to read about?" I pointed out to Molly.

"Yes," she sulked, slumping down on her bed. "I bet you get to travel again, don't you?"

"Maybe," I smirked, going back to my file.

"You and Georgie always get to travel." Molly let out a deep sigh before pulling her own target information out to read up on.

* * *

"Oh, God...yes, Jade!" I was slowly riding up and down

on Mr. Manning's less than impressive length. His divorce had ended badly this year, and his wife was very bitter. She'd paid for a Seductor to steal her diamond necklace that he had been awarded by the courts, as an extra payment for his betrayal. A woman scorned and all that crap, I guess. The necklace was valued at over one hundred thousand dollars, so I could see why she wanted it. I was sure the ex-Mrs. Manning would get over his treachery once she'd gotten her diamonds back.

"I can't believe how turned on you make me," I moaned, arching my back as I pushed harder against him. These men were all the same. You could fuck them senseless and then steal their whole life while they slept. It was so easy.

"I can't believe I've only known you for three days," Mr. Manning panted as he moved his hands up to my lace covered breasts. I forced a grin, moving them away. I didn't like to be touched if I could help it. I was still more or less fully clothed, too. I'd just hitched my skirt up and opened my top, wanting to make this quick so I could start planning for my mission with Mr. Kirkham.

"Let me do the touching," I smoldered, pushing his arms behind his head on the pillows. "If you still have the energy once I'm finished, you can touch me *anywhere* you want." Mr. Manning nodded, groaning as I began to slam down onto him, moving my hand behind me to play with his balls. By the time I was done, he wouldn't be able to move and I'd be able to take the diamond necklace from his safe. I'd be gone before he even awoke.

Another mission completed, and yet somehow, I knew my next mission wasn't going to be quite this easy.

* * *

I'd only touched down in London a few hours ago, but I was already perched on a stool at the exclusive Savoy Hotel Bar where Mr. Kirkham was staying. I'd opted for a simple black cocktail dress, which showed off my ample cleavage perfectly. I was lucky—I had curves in all the right places and was able to drive the men wild. My breasts were debatably one of my best assets, and completely natural. After curling my hair, I'd pulled half of it back and pinned it in place. I was touching my lipstick up when my target finally arrived in the bar.

His picture really didn't do him any justice. As he glided through the room effortlessly, he shook hands with a few people he must have known. He looked younger than his photo, but then I had read that he was only thirty-two.

I suspected a lot of the people in the bar would be attending the industrial conference that he was leading this weekend. That was going to make it difficult for me to try and get him alone, but not impossible.

The first contact with a target was always about observation—watching for any threats, taking note of their favorite drink, being ready for that first connection, and lastly, making sure you were the actual sex the target was attracted to. I'd been there once before and I can tell you now, I may have been good at my job, but I wasn't *that* good.

Mr. Kirkham definitely liked the ladies. I watched his hands linger on a few attractive women numerous times in the first hour I sat watching him.

For a rich man, I was shocked to discover his preferred

drink was a bottle of lager, but then again, maybe he was just trying to relax. Lager was a lighter drink than liquor.

He seemed to have the gift of conversation, too, and I'd be lying if I didn't admit I was looking forward to meeting him.

"Can I buy you a drink, Beautiful?" I heard the guy sitting next to me ask. I sighed, trying not to roll my eyes at the drunken idiot.

"I'm good, thank you," I smiled, turning my stool away from him. I was trying to work here!

Men were all the same. They would see a woman alone and instantly think it was an opportunity to try and pick her up. I never was a woman you could chat up, even before I found this job.

"You're here alone, aren't you?" he whispered into my ear while his chest rubbed against my back. He really shouldn't have been doing that. He wouldn't like it if I got angry.

"Hey, Jackass! What part of '*I'm good, thank you*,' don't you understand?" I seethed, spinning in my seat. The guy was no oil painting, either. He didn't stand a chance with me in the slightest.

"I don't like seeing a beautiful woman drink alone," he slurred.

"Trust me, if it's a choice between drinking with you or alone, I'm fine with being alone."

"Hey!" The guy was about to grab my shoulder, and I'd have floored him if he had, but luckily we were interrupted.

"Mark, you're not harassing the ladies again, are you?" I turned and came face-to-face with Mr. Kirkham, himself. *Oh my!* He was rather dreamy up close. Sonia was right: a few months with this guy wouldn't be so bad. I may even be able to teach him a thing or two and finally get an orgasm out of it—*without* having to use my own fingers for once. Maybe it was the men I had been assigned to, or the knowledge that the connection wasn't real, but never in my five years as a Seductor had a target brought me to orgasm. *Why was I thinking about orgasms already?* I hadn't even spoken to the man yet.

"She was insulting me, actually, Oliver!" Mr. Drunk mumbled, glaring daggers at me.

"I merely said I didn't need a drink after your kind offer. If I had insulted you, I would have said your breath smelled or that color shirt looks ridiculous on you," I replied, watching Mr. Kirkham's eyes lighten with humor.

"I still think you should let me buy you a drink," Mr. Drunk sneered, trying unsuccessfully to be seductive.

"I'd really rather you didn't," I whimpered, using my innocent approach. *Oh, Mr. Kirkham, save me! I'm just a poor little girl that needs to be protected.*

The truth was, I was going to seduce the pants off Mr. Kirkham over the next few months. Hell, who knew? I might even be able to start tonight.

"Mark, leave the poor woman alone," he scolded. "You'll have to excuse Mark." Mr. Kirkham was now giving me his full attention, gazing at me with those brown, almost black, eyes of his. Using that to my advantage, I crossed my legs and gave him a great view of my upper thigh. I leaned in closer to him, too, knowing it would show my cleavage off nicely. "I can ask him to leave if you want."

"Are you always this heroic?" I asked, looking away and acting shy.

"Only for extremely beautiful women," he grinned.

"You're making me blush," I giggled, running my fingers over the top of my glass, silently teasing him. He was a man, after all, and I knew he was already picturing me naked, hoping he could run his own hands all over me.

"I'm sorry. That wasn't my intention, I was just stating the truth." Mr. Kirkham took the stool next to me, which luckily blocked my view of the drunk guy.

"Do you charm all the ladies this way?"

"*All* the ladies?" he asked, quirking an eyebrow at me.

"I've been watching you tonight. You seem quite the celebrity," I sighed.

"You've been watching *me*?" he chuckled. "And here I was thinking I'd spotted you first." I giggled, adding in that hair flick thing girls do when they're nervous. I had this act down to a fine art. "Can *I* buy you a drink?"

"I can't see any harm in that. You did save me, after all," I smiled, finally looking up to meet his gaze. Oh, he was making this too easy. "I'll have a bottle of lager, thanks."

"Lager?" he questioned. *Rule #11 : Seductors must always order the same drink as their target on their first contact. This is to ensure a commonality and provide an in for the first official meet.*

"What? You think all women drink cocktails? Don't you ever get sick of conforming with everyone else?"

"Two bottles of lager it is, then," he smiled, tilting his head. "I just realized I haven't introduced myself. I'm Oliver Kirkham."

"It's lovely to meet you, Oliver. I'm Jade—Jade Gibbs." We always gave our real first name. It was easier that way. A Seductor never handled the same target more than once, so it was safe.

"It's lovely to meet you, too, Jade." Oliver smiled, passing my drink to me once the bartender set them down. "Here's to new acquaintances." I nodded, clinking my bottle with his.

"So what brings you to London?" he asked after a sip of his beer. "I can tell by your accent that you're not local."

"Neither are you," I pointed out, knowing full well he was an American like me. "I'm here on business," I continued.

"What part of the US are you from?"

"Florida. I'm in the interior design business—artwork mainly. I look for certain pieces for my clients, and London has it all." It was good to have a cover story that you actually knew about, and I was a big art lover. It was one of my many disguises.

"That sounds interesting."

"What type of business are you in, Mr. Kirkham?" I asked, sipping my beer while gazing up at him with my big blue eyes.

"It's *Oliver*. I'm in the industrial business, mostly," he grinned. A few people acknowledged him as they passed, but Oliver kept his eyes on me.

"What does that mean exactly?"

"I run a company that makes machines of all kinds."

"Oh." I acted shocked.

"What?" he questioned as his eyes started to roam down toward my chest.

"You don't seem old enough to run your own company."

"Oh, I'm old enough, but I'm also a third generation CEO, so I can't take *all* the credit," he chuckled, turning to greet a few more people. "You must have done well in your career, too, Jade. You can't be more than what—twenty-five?"

"You're close," I smirked. "I'm twenty-seven." I was impressed. Age wasn't an easy thing to guess with me.

"Mm…you're not too far from my age," he mused, licking his lip subconsciously.

"Can I try to guess how old *you* are?"

"If you want," he smiled playfully. I already knew his age, of course, but Oliver didn't know that.

"Thirty…" I paused, pretending to think as I gazed at him. Damn, Oliver was really a good looking guy. "Thirty-four," I finally guessed.

"Close," he chuckled, "but you added an extra two years."

"Clearly the stress of your job has added two years onto you," I teased into my bottle.

"You could be right there, Jade."

"Well, everyone seems to know you in this bar. You must be someone important, that's for sure," I mused, looking around.

"I'm heading up a conference here this weekend."

"Ah," I giggled, "it all makes sense now."

"How long are you in London?" I noticed his gaze had moved to my exposed leg and was traveling up my thigh.

"Just the weekend. I'm meeting with a new client in Paris on Monday."

"You're here for the same amount of time as me, then," he stated.

"It would seem so," I smiled, playing with the hem of my dress timidly. I couldn't appear too confident. Oliver seemed to like my '*lost little girl*' act.

"Do you usually travel alone in your line of work?"

"No, this is my first time," I sighed, taking another sip of my drink. "Our company has taken on a lot of new clients. There aren't enough of us to go around anymore, so I had to take this job alone. It's all a little daunting."

"Don't you have a boyfriend or husband who could have come with you?" *Oh, smooth, Oliver—really smooth.*

"No," I sighed sadly. "No husband or boyfriend."

"I wouldn't be so worried about being in London alone. You seem to be doing just fine from where I'm sitting, Jade."

"Thank you."

"So, are you meeting a client tonight?"

"I was supposed to," I sighed deeply, "but unfortunately he had to cancel. I was just about to decide what to do for the evening."

"You mean you're all dressed up with nowhere to go?" Oliver stood up. "We can't have that. Why don't you join me for dinner in the restaurant?"

"Oh, Oliver, I couldn't. I...I mean, you probably have a hundred things to do."

"No, I don't, actually. Right now, I'd like to take a very beautiful woman to dinner." He certainly was a charmer, I had to give him that.

"Well, when you put it that way, how can I resist?" I beamed, taking the hand he offered to me.

Oliver wined and dined me with style. The conversation followed effortlessly, and a few hours later we were back in the bar having a nightcap.

"I really can't thank you enough for dinner, Oliver."

"It was my pleasure, Jade. I've enjoyed your companionship immensely tonight."

"Do you really own your own company?"

"Why do you ask that?" he chuckled into his coffee.

"You're so young and...*fun*. I thought CEOs were supposed to be bald with beer bellies, and be too stressed out to even crack a smile."

"Are those the kind of CEOs you have as your clients?"

"Yes," I laughed.

"These interior art skills of yours—how much do they cost?"

"Are you interested in utilizing my skills, Oliver?"

"I'm very interested, Miss Gibbs." Oliver's look became almost predatory.

"Maybe we should take this conversation elsewhere, then?" I suggested, looking around the bar.

"Where did you have in mind?" he asked, moving a little closer, his hand lightly skimming my leg.

"I was thinking of retiring for the night. It's getting quite late," I breathed, stretching out to play with his tie.

"Alone?"

"Actually, I was kind of hoping for some company," I whispered timidly, pushing off my stool and slowly walking toward the lobby area. Counting to five, I turned to see Oliver walking toward me, looking dark and dangerously handsome. I was actually looking forward to seeing if this guy was any good in bed.

I pushed the button for the elevator and leaned against the wall just as he caught up with me.

"I hope I'm reading these signs correctly," he grinned just as the elevator doors opened. With a small grin, I stepped in and pulled him with me. Oliver crashed his lips against mine right as the doors closed behind us.

Kissing was second nature to me. I could fake desire, even if it felt like I was kissing a wet fish, but as Oliver lifted me by my ass and pinned me against the elevator wall, I groaned in *actual* pleasure. I didn't have to fake it. Desire flooded through my veins as I ran my hands into his dark hair.

"Christ, you're beautiful," he groaned, his lips moving down my neck while his hands began to fumble for the hem of my dress. I was about to start dry humping the guy if he kept on like he was.

"Ugh..." I groaned as his hands worked their way under my dress and he gripped my ass cheeks roughly. "Oliver...ugh... which floor?" He leaned toward the elevator buttons with me still wrapped around him, and pressed a button before quickly returning to attacking my neck.

"I saw you the moment I walked into the bar tonight," he purred, his hands running slowly down my chest. Both my legs were wrapped around his waist. "And I wanted you."

"Ugh...I...I'm flattered," I said, forcing a blush. The elevator opened and Oliver finally let me go. As I slid down his body, I could feel his muscles through his shirt. Mm...it really was going to be a fun few months.

"I want you to know I don't usually do this sort of thing," I muttered, playing with the zipper on my purse while he opened his bedroom door.

"Neither do I." He shook his head as if to clear it from a random thought, and somehow, I didn't believe him. He was too smooth and confident to have never picked a girl up in a bar before.

"Wow, your room is so much bigger than mine!" I acted awestruck, gazing around as I placed my bag on a table. "Is this just the living area?" I gasped, turning to see that he was suddenly right in front of me. He responded by crashing his lips against mine while backing me against the wall.

"I don't want to make small talk anymore. I just want to fuck you, Jade," he growled into my ear. Holy crap! I was so turned on; I could feel the wetness between my legs begin to flow. His hands came back up underneath my dress, but rather than grab my ass like he had in the elevator, he simply pulled my panties down. "Do you want me to fuck you?"

"YES!" It was a plea, because in that moment, I'd never wanted anything more. I heard his belt buckle and the sound of foil before he was suddenly slamming me hard against the wall. Fuck, I'd dreamed of being taken this way, but never once had I thought it would happen. Who was this guy?

"I'm going to make you cum harder than you've ever cum before," he smoldered into my ear. His fingers slowly teased my entrance and I arched my back, needing more. "I can feel how much you want this. I know your kind—shy and withdrawn. Let me free you. Let me release the desire I know is inside you." Oh, this guy had no idea just how much *desire* was inside me. I wrapped my legs tightly around his waist, drawing him toward me before I bit down on his neck.

"Fuck, yes," Oliver growled, and with one deep thrust he was inside me.

I'd never been fucked this hard before. I was wanton. I needed everything the guy could give me as he slammed into me over and over again while I was pinned against the wall. "You feel so good," he panted between thrusts.

"Fuck me harder!" I was totally breaking character, but I'd never had a man bring me to orgasm without my help before, and right now, I needed that moment more than the air I breathed.

"Harder? You better brace yourself then." Oliver gripped

my legs and rotated his hips before pushing deeper and faster inside me.

Before I could make sense of what was happening, I felt myself begin to build—the feeling becoming warmer and more intense with each of his movements. This guy was going to make me cum. Jade Phillips—top Seductor—was finally going to cum by the power of a man!

"Give it to me, Jade. Don't you fucking dare deny yourself!" Oliver could feel my orgasm begin to take control, so he slid his fingers between us, circling my clit to help ease my release out.

When I did explode, it was earth shattering.

"Ugh...fuck...fuck...fuck," I groaned, my entire body trembling.

Oliver continued to pound into me until he found his own release. "Fuck, yes, Jade...ugh...ugh...I knew you'd make me cum this hard!" Oh my God! He looked so hot when he climaxed.

I was still pinned against the wall, held up by his arms as we regulated our breathing.

"You see?" Oliver finally spoke. "I knew there was a wild girl in there somewhere."

Oh, Oliver, you have no idea.

CHAPTER TWO

My legs were a little wobbly as Oliver finally led me into his bedroom.

"Wow, this bedroom is something else," I gasped when he turned the bedside lights on. He'd pulled his trousers back up, but they were still partly open and I had to fight the urge to lick my lips. I was desperate to fuck this guy again now that he'd just made me cum harder than ever before, but something told me from our time against the living room wall, that Oliver liked to take the lead in the bedroom.

"You didn't really come here to look at the interior of this bedroom, did you, Jade?" His voice was husky as he pulled me back into his arms. "I was hoping you were here for something else."

"If it's more of what just happened out there, then yes, that's exactly what I'm here for." I closed my eyes as I felt his hands begin to undo the clasp on my dress.

Very slowly, Oliver began to pull it down my body. I wasn't wearing any panties, and I suspected they were still on the floor in the living area somewhere.

"Christ, you're perfect," he said as he gazed at me in awe. His hands ran down my back before he cupped my ass.

I was standing before him in just my black lace bra, and I could feel my body begin to burn with need again. I wasn't sure who was playing whom at the moment.

I held my breath, fighting back a moan as he moved behind me and gripped my breasts firmly in his hands. "I'm going to take this one slow. You're going to feel *everything*, Jade." Oh, that sounded glorious, and yet I tried to reason with my mind—wasn't I supposed to be seducing him and not the other way around?

I could take the night off and just lose myself, couldn't I? It would be well deserved. I'd get back on the case tomorrow. Tonight, I just wanted to come alive under this man's touch.

I felt his hands undo the clasp on my bra, and gently, he pushed it off my shoulders so it fell to the floor.

"Go and lie down on the bed on your back," he whispered with a voice like pure velvet. I did as I was told, which was a first for me. *Me taking orders from a man—what was the world coming to?*

His eyes raked over me while he began to undress. "You are one hell of a sight, Jade," he smoldered. I giggled almost hysterically at how this situation had changed. I was lying here, waiting for this man to take me to the deepest depths of pleasure. Why wasn't my mind on the job? "Close your eyes," he ordered as he undid his shirt. Now I was pissed! I wanted to see his body first, but I still followed his instructions.

A few moments later, I felt the bed move and knew Oliver must have joined me. "Keep those eyes closed until I say so, Jade." I heard his voice just as he parted my legs.

Damn, with my eyes closed, I could *feel* everything.

His hands slowly ran down both my legs; his touch was

sending my body into a frenzy. He made his way up my body and began grazing my ribcage with his fingertips; his touches were so different than before in the living room. They were feather light, but just as intense.

When he finally palmed my breasts, pulling slightly on my hardened nipples, I groaned and arched up to him.

"Oh, Baby, you really have a lot of sexual frustration to release, don't you? I can help you with that." I thought this guy was an industrial CEO—not a sex expert.

"Ugh…please, Oliver," I yearned, fisting the sheets behind me as I felt his hot mouth clamp down on my right nipple.

"Keep those eyes shut," he breathed, moving to lavish my other nipple. "I promise you won't regret it." It was difficult not to obey him while he was playing with my body so well. "Jade, you have no idea how much I want you," he snarled, biting down on my nipple as he sucked it into his mouth. "You're everything I've ever wanted in a woman and more." He knew that just from one night with me? *Damn, I was good.*

I felt him use his body to part my legs more as his hands slowly trickled further down my stomach. I was gasping, waiting for his fingers to touch me where I needed him the most.

"I can feel how much you want this," he murmured against my ear as his fingers began to make small circles against my entrance. "Do you want this, Jade?" Oliver asked, pushing against my opening.

"YES!" I wasn't sure if it was an answer or a plea, but I felt him chuckle against my skin before he slowly began to ease his fingers in and out of me.

"Can you feel that?" Oh, I really could. I nodded, catching my breath as his lips descended on my nipple again. His attack was relentless. I was squirming and yet I needed more. I wanted it faster, but when I began to beg, it only made him go slower.

"Just feel it, Jade," he cooed. "You'll get there...enjoy the journey." His voice was pure sex and I knew immediately what he meant. I was becoming wetter and wetter with every second, and could feel a small fire in the pit of my stomach. It *was* happening; I just needed to be patient.

Oliver shifted on the bed, and I felt his body cover mine while he was still working me with his fingers. He was naked, and his cool flesh against my heated skin felt incredible.

"Mm...let's awaken that desire again, shall we?" he purred into my neck. I was panting as I felt him kiss his way down my body. *Oh, please say he was heading where I thought he was!*

When I felt his lips against my stomach, I called out his name almost like a prayer.

"I love the way my name sounds coming from your lips, Jade." Desperate to open my eyes at that moment, I felt his shoulders shift my legs further apart. Oh, he was... Before I could even finish my thoughts, he'd parted my folds and had taken a long, slow lick against my clit.

"Argh!" My eyes snapped open from the pleasure racing around my body.

"Hush now," he soothed from between my legs. "And those eyes better still be closed. You'll feel *this* more, I promise."

"Jesus—Oliver, what are you *doing* to me?" That was the real me asking. I could feel him chuckle against my heat before he sucked my clit into his mouth. Forcing my eyes shut, I became a slave to his touch.

He alternated between licking and sucking my clit, and when he began to insert his fingers into my entrance, I could feel the burning in my stomach begin to rise.

"Oh...Oh...Oliver!" I was thrashing against his mouth, my orgasm hitting me like a freight train. My hands found his hair and I gripped it tightly while he coaxed me through my climax with his tongue.

Having never felt so completely spent before, I couldn't even open my eyes. I could feel Oliver's lips make their way back up my body while I tried to regain some sense of normality.

"You can open your eyes now," he purred when his lips were against my neck.

"Who the hell are you?" I gasped, gazing into his dark, lustful eyes when I opened mine.

"I'm Oliver Kirkham. We met downstairs earlier, remember?" he teased, stroking my face.

"Oliver, I've never...and I mean *never* had an experience as intense as that before."

"Business isn't the only thing I'm good at," he winked, leaning down to capture my lips with his. I could taste myself on him and groaned. Christ, it was beyond hot! "I've never been this physically attracted to anyone before, either. Jade, I want to devour you." His hands ran down the left side of my body and I was helpless, lost in his words as he continued. "Will you let me devour you? You have no idea how much my body is aching for you." All I could do was nod as I gave in, giving Oliver complete control over me.

It was just one night. Tomorrow I would get back to the real reason I was here.

"I want to worship you all night," he whispered, hovering over me before stretching to grab a condom. As he did so, I finally got a chance to look at his naked form. I'd been right, Oliver had an amazing body, and I was looking forward to getting my hands on it.

"Is that a promise?" I giggled, wriggling underneath him once he was back on top of me.

"If your client doesn't mind you falling asleep at your meeting tomorrow, I could arrange that."

"What about you? Aren't you here for a conference? You need your sleep, too."

"I can live on four hours of sleep a night." Oliver moved to look at his clock on his nightstand before putting the condom on his impressive length. I couldn't believe *that* had been inside me; no wonder I felt so full. "By my calculations, I have another three hours until I need to go to sleep," he teased, grinding his erection against my entrance.

"Three hours sounds good to me," I beamed, wrapping my arms around his neck.

"Maybe even four," Oliver smirked, leaning down to capture my lips with his. As his tongue darted in to meet mine, I felt his hands lift my hips up, and with one swift motion he was inside me again.

We both groaned at how good it felt. Oliver began to pound into me at a fast pace while I clung to him. I couldn't make sense of anything. All I knew was that I never wanted this night to end.

I lay in the darkness hours later, staring into space. What the hell had just happened?
Targets weren't supposed to be this amazing, especially after only the first connection. I fought with the feelings inside my head all night as I struggled to sleep. My judgment had been so

clouded by my lust for this man.

I wasn't attached—not yet, anyway—but I could see that happening if I let this sex-driven side of me control the mission.

Oliver was an incredible lover.

He was rough *and* gentle, and that was a dangerous mix. Hell, he was the male version of me in the bedroom. I couldn't let him see that side of me now; otherwise, my cover would be blown.

Oliver had been attracted to the shy, innocent wallflower that had been perched at the bar—not the hellcat I really was. Shy Jade was the character I needed to be from this moment on.

Somehow, I had to force the real me back and concentrate on the job at hand. I should have been thankful. At least I was going to get two months of amazing sex out of this, as well as my salary for the mission.

I just had to make sure I stayed focused.

I stretched to find the bed empty when I woke up. I don't think my body had ever felt so relaxed, but that might have had something to do with all the orgasms last night. I lost count after number seven.

Wrapping one of the sheets from the bed around myself, I went in search of Oliver. His suite was huge; I'd checked two rooms before I found him showered and dressed, eating breakfast at the dining room table.

"I was just about to wake you. Would you care for some breakfast?" He gestured toward the spread in front of him.

"Um...I might just take a shower. I'm not really a breakfast person." Why was I being so truthful with him?

"Jade, breakfast is the most important meal of the day," he tutted. "Won't you at least have some tea or coffee?"

"Coffee sounds good," I smiled, taking a seat and wrapping the sheet tighter around my body. I don't know why I was so self-conscious. Oliver had seen it *all* last night—in great detail, I might add.

"How are you feeling?" he asked as he poured me a cup of the steaming hot liquid.

"Very relaxed," I giggled, running my hands through my hair. Damn, I should have brushed it before I came looking for him.

"I wonder why that is," Oliver winked, stretching to pick up his phone to check. "Excuse me for a second, Jade. I won't be but a moment." I nodded as I watched him walk out onto the balcony to make a call.

I needed to ensure a second date before I left this morning. There was no doubt that Oliver would want to see me again, but I had to push aside the fact *I* wanted to see *him* again.

"Sorry about that," he said, snapping me out of my thoughts. "My office never sleeps."

"It's fine," I smiled shyly, trying to get back into character. I came here to do a job—a job I was good at. Damn it, I wouldn't allow myself to fall for his charms!

"What are your plans for later?" Oliver asked, tilting my chin up so he could look me in the eyes.

"I'll be meeting my client this afternoon."

"What about after?"

"I don't have any plans."

"Well, you do now," he grinned, leaning down to peck my lips. "Last night was…incredible. Thank you."

"I feel as if *I* should be thanking *you*," I exhaled. "I never knew it could be that intense."

"It's all about reading what your body wants." Oliver's eyes were growing dark with lust, and I held the sheet tighter around my body, trying to control the desire that was seeping through my veins. "For instance," he continued, taking my hand and making me stand, "right now, I can tell you want me to touch you."

"H…how can you tell?"

"Your breathing is deeper." Smirking, he moved my hand that was holding onto the sheet. "You keep swallowing, trying to control what you're denying yourself," he whispered, undoing the thin material and letting it drop to the floor so I was standing naked before him. "And now I see the evidence," he chuckled, running his thumbs over my hard nipples before dipping his hand lower into my dripping wet sex. "Oh Jade, I can read you so well already," Oliver smoldered, leaning down to attack one of my nipples with his mouth while his fingers moved in and out of me. I braced myself, using the table to try and stay upright while attempting to adjust to his sudden attack. He had me yelling out his name within minutes.

"You're so desirable, Jade," he groaned into my ear. I couldn't even speak. "Will you let me take you out to dinner tonight?" He slowly removed his fingers from inside me as he asked the question.

"Yes," I gasped, trying to catch my breath. Oliver grinned and then pecked my lips.

"I need to get going, but help yourself to anything you'd like, and you're welcome to take a shower here if you want. I'll meet you at the bar tonight. Let's say…seven?"

"That sounds perfect," I beamed. Oliver kissed me once more, and with a smirk on his face, he left. He didn't even wash his hands. Why did I find that so *hot*?

I smiled to myself—alone in his bedroom already. Oliver Kirkham really made it too easy for me. After I had a shower and got changed, I began snooping around his things; I knew I probably wouldn't get lucky the first time. The blueprints I was looking for were top secret, after all, but even a hint of where the hard drive might be was a start.

I attempted to access his laptop but couldn't. I'd need to work on gaining his passwords for all his computer files first. The only paper files in his room were all related to the industrial conference that he was heading this weekend, so I was out of luck there, too.

With a deep sigh, I gave up. There was nothing here.

I checked in with headquarters when I got back to my room, letting them know I'd made first contact with the target and had secured a second date this evening.

"What's he like?" Sonia asked.

"Very professional," I lied. I couldn't really tell her the truth—that Oliver was the most amazing lover I'd ever had.

"Where did you spend last night?"

"In his bed."

"Good girl. Keep me informed." With that, Sonia hung up.

After the phone call, I got myself ready for the day. I still had to play the part of an interior art designer even though I wasn't one. All Seductors had proof of their fake identities, including business cards, a working office that was really directed back to headquarters, and fake backgrounds that would be found if the target did a check. Of course, we had a different identity for each case, too; nothing was ever left to chance. There was a reason *The Seductors* were at the top of their game. It was because of the detailed planning that was done before any mission was undertaken.

Having not been in years, I spent my afternoon touring around London, and I had to admit the shopping was amazing. I lost track of the hours I spent on Oxford Street.

I returned to the hotel later that afternoon loaded down with bags. I may have gone a little overboard, but I knew Oliver was taking me out to dinner tonight, so I had to buy a new cocktail dress. That, of course, meant I needed new shoes. Then I thought: why not go the whole way with some sexy underwear? That would drive him crazy.

I needed to up my game tonight and take control of this situation, and my outfit was just the beginning.

CHAPTER THREE

Oliver arrived at the bar later that night, looking more dashing than the night before in a custom tailored, gray striped suit.

"You look stunning, Jade," he smiled, pulling me close to his body as he kissed my cheek. I could feel his hands graze down my bare back and knew I'd chosen my dress well; it was already driving him wild. The red dress was *very* short and *very* tight, and the thin, crisscrossing straps were the only material on my back. I got the feeling Oliver liked that a lot. "I've been thinking about you all day," he whispered, stroking my arms softly. It was time to play the game; I'd had my fun last night, but now I needed to get to work.

"I've been thinking about you all day, too," I muttered, not meeting his gaze. I was trying to play the shy, insecure woman he wanted.

Oliver tilted my chin and I was met with his blistering gaze. "Don't be afraid of your feelings, Jade."

"I've only known you for a day, Oliver. I can't trust them right now."

"Why not?" he frowned, still cupping my face.

"You've awakened feelings in me I never knew existed, and I'm afraid of what tomorrow will bring. We both leave in the morning."

"You think I won't want to see you once we're back in America?" Oliver smirked, his thumb slowly running over my lips. I parted them with a gasp; this man's touch was something else. I could feel the inferno from last night begin to burn me from the inside out. "Come on, let me take you to dinner. We have much to discuss." He took my hand in his and led me outside to a waiting limo.

"Are you trying to impress me, Oliver?" I giggled, hitting his chest playfully.

"Is it working?"

"A little," I grinned before stepping into the limo. I was definitely impressed. It seemed that Oliver had gone all out tonight, with soft music playing in the background, champagne chilling in a glass ice bucket, and two polished glasses waiting to be filled. "Oh my," I giggled as he joined me. "I'm not used to this sort of treatment."

"You should be. Jade, you deserve to be worshiped every single day," Oliver murmured against my ear before moving to open the champagne.

"I don't know what to say to that," I blushed, playing with the hem of my dress. *Oh, poor little insecure Jade.* Judging by the way Oliver was watching me, he was falling for it, too.

"How was your meeting?" he asked, handing me a glass of champagne.

"Fine. I showed my clients a few pieces by Pierre Dubois. He's a new name in modern art. They may make an offer on two of the paintings I suggested."

"Have you always had a passion for art?" he asked with interest. I smiled, watching Oliver undo his jacket buttons and get comfortable in the back of the limo.

"Yes. I always wanted to have a job that involved my passion. Art means a lot to me."

"Do you think you might have room on your client list for me?"

"You really want to utilize my time?" I gasped. "I thought that was just a trick to get me into your bed."

Oliver's eyes became hungry as he raked them over my body. "We *could* have these discussions in my bed. I wouldn't be opposed to that," he smoldered, lightly tracing my leg with his fingertips.

"I'm not sure I'd get any work done," I mused, sipping my champagne.

"Mm...you might be right," Oliver smiled, leaning in to capture my lips with his. I almost dropped the glass I was holding when his tongue darted into my mouth and slowly began to dance with mine. Shit, he could really kiss. I tried to fight back the desire, but it was already filling every inch of my body. "Maybe I should take this," he chuckled, grabbing the glass from me and placing it, along with his own, on the small bar. He then pushed a button that made a privacy screen slide up, blocking the driver's view of us. "Mm...that's better." While pulling me toward him, his hands began pushing my dress up around my thighs. "Fuck, you have amazing legs." With a groan, he grabbed me roughly. I threw my head back when I felt his fingers sweep over my panty-covered sex. "You have no idea how much I want you right now." Oliver's voice was hoarse and full of obvious desire.

"I think I have an idea," I forced out as his lips began to make their way down my neck.

"I promised myself I would wine and dine you first."

"I really don't mind," I whimpered as he began making small circles over my panties.

"You're not making this easy for me." Oliver thrust himself into me and I could feel his erection rub against my leg. *Oh yes, please!* Limo sex sounded wonderful! "I need to ask that we make a little detour," he smirked, picking up the intercom. Once he had asked the driver to continue driving until he said so, his attention was focused solely on me.

"First," Oliver panted, going for the zipper on my dress, "I need you naked."

"Then what are you waiting for?" I purred, pushing him back against the seat. With one swift movement, he was pulling my dress over my head and I was straddling his lap in just my panties.

"Mm...I like you being on top, Jade," he beamed. His lips were quick to latch onto my right nipple while his hands worked to remove my panties. In a matter of seconds, I was naked in the back of the limo, straddling an insanely hot guy. *I've told you how much I love my job, right?*

I worked Oliver's slacks open and freed his steel cock. Christ, he was already leaking—so ready for me. Why did that turn me on so much? Oliver was *just* a target.

"Are you going to ride my cock, Beautiful?" he panted, biting my earlobe.

"I want to," I whispered, "but I'm afraid. Will you help me?" I pleaded with my innocent eyes.

"Of course I will," he grinned, running his hand through my hair softly. Oh, he was putty in my hands. *Just you wait, Mr. Kirkham; I'm about to make you fall harder than you ever thought possible.*

I smiled shyly as I rubbed my drenched center over his erection. Oliver threw his head back, gritting his teeth. "Don't forget the condom, Jade," he groaned as I rotated my hips once more.

"Where are they?" I asked, licking down his neck.

"Fuck...in my wallet. Back...fuck...back pocket." Oliver lifted his hips, allowing me to slide his wallet out of the back pocket of his partly open pants.

When I ripped the condom open with my teeth, I thought he was going to explode. Instead, he began to devour my breasts, sucking and nibbling on them as if he were a starving man.

I rolled the rubber over his impressive length once I'd opened his pants more, and groaned because my action caused Oliver to bite down hard on my left nipple.

"Sorry, Baby," he purred, licking the sore spot before pulling me over his hard cock. "Fuck...Jade, you are so sexy."

"You'll help me, won't you?" I asked again, running my hands through his hair.

"You will feel amazing no matter what you do, Jade. You have no idea how much you turn me on."

"I kind of have an idea," I giggled, pushing against his hard cock. Oliver groaned, grabbing my ass and holding me still while he composed himself.

"Don't tease me, Jade, or I'll end up fucking you so raw you won't walk for a week." *Fuck, that was hot!* I grinned, slowly sinking down onto his length while staring into his dark scorching eyes. "Oh, that's it. Fuck...yes," he moaned. His fingers were digging into my ass cheeks now, but it felt wonderful.

I quickly undid his tie and opened his shirt so part of his

chest was visible. "Mm…" I purred, raking my nails down his chest as I slowly rose up and down on his length.

"That's it, Jade," he encouraged, guiding me with his hands. In a few moments I'd give him everything I had, but I wanted to build up to that. I was poor little shy Jade, after all. "Fuck—you feel *so* good."

I braced myself, grabbing onto the seat behind him as I began to rock my hips faster. Oliver moaned, his hands moving up to palm my breast as I started to really fuck him, rotating my hips so I could take him in all the way. I threw my head back and became a slave to the desire. I wanted to feel him twitch inside me. I wanted to cum on that glorious cock of his.

"Holy shit, Jade," Oliver mumbled, grabbing my hair and kissing me feverishly while I continued to ride him hard. His hands were frantically roaming over my body, and I smiled in satisfaction as I felt him begin to twitch within me.

Oliver came hard, holding me close with his head buried between my breasts.

"How was that?" I giggled innocently when he finally looked up and withdrew himself from me.

"I knew there was sex goddess inside you somewhere," he snarled before dipping his fingers into my heated center. As his fingers ran over my clit, I suppressed a groan. "But you forgot something important," he smirked, leaning down to bite my right nipple. I felt myself get wetter as he teased it with his tongue and teeth. "A goddess needs to climax, too." With a few flicks of his finger, I felt myself begin to build. *How did he do that so quickly?* "Give it to me, Jade. Then I'll take you to dinner," he growled, working me faster. Oh, pure pleasure was beginning to shoot through every nerve ending in my body. "Stop holding back. I can feel you trying to deny yourself," he ordered. Damn it, I was supposed to be controlling myself this time. I gave in with three more flicks of his fingers and fell into the abyss, moaning out his name.

"Why do you do that?" he whispered against my neck, holding me close to his body.

"Do what?" I panted, catching my breath.

"Deny your body what it clearly wants." Oliver smiled sadly, tucking my hair behind my ears.

"I wasn't aware I was doing that," I lied, running my fingers against the exposed part of his chest.

"You're quite the mystery, Jade," he mused while watching me.

"No, I'm not. I'm just your average working class woman, trying to make her way in this world," I sighed. The look on Oliver's face was disapproving.

"*Average*? Jade, you're the most beautiful woman I have ever seen. Can't you see the effect you've had on me already?" he scolded. "And the way you just rode me...fuck. It's making me hard again to just think about it." I giggled, feeling his erection press against my stomach.

"You need to feed me before we go again. I'm not sure I'll have the energy to keep up otherwise."

"Okay," he chuckled, finally releasing me so I could slide off his lap. My clothes were scattered all over the limo, so I set about gathering everything. It didn't take Oliver long to get redressed and remove the evidence of our lovemaking. Then again, he hadn't been fully undressed like I was.

"Why was I the only naked one in the back of this limo?" I smiled as he helped me zip my dress back up.

"I was in too much of a rush to get my hands on that body of yours to get undressed," Oliver replied truthfully. "Naked Jade is an amazing sight to behold." *Damn,* he was such a smooth talker.

"You always know just what to say to make me blush."

"You're a beautiful woman, Jade. You must know that," he muttered, kissing my lips softly.

"I've never had a man as dashing as you who was interested in me before."

"I'm *more* than just interested," he smoldered, crashing his lips passionately against mine. *Mr. Kirkham, you are making this too easy.*

Oliver and I finally made it to dinner. He took me to a charming little fine dining restaurant in Knightsbridge, where we were seated at a candlelit table for two near the window.

"Have you been to this restaurant before?" I asked, looking over the menu.

"What are you trying to say?" he smirked, watching me.

"I know what *this* is, Oliver. I bet you have a string of women all over the world that come running when you touch down in their city." It was time to work out what kind of a man Oliver Kirkham really was. "And that's fine, just as long as I know and don't fall any deeper than I already have. It's been a truly amazing weekend—one that I will never forget."

"You think this is just about *one* weekend?" Oliver gasped sharply. "Jade, I have never had this level of connection with anyone before—mentally *or* physically. You are perfect for me."

"What are you saying?" I frowned.

"I want to see you again after this weekend."

"You do?" I sucked in a deep breath, acting completely

shocked.

"You really can't see what you've done to me, can you?" I shook my head, looking down at the table to avoid eye contact. "I'm bewitched by you, Jade Gibbs." The bewilderment in his voice made me snap my eyes back up to him. Christ, Oliver was good.

"I don't know how it would work. How would we see each other back home?"

"We'll make it work. For starters, I plan on hiring you for your services," he winked, licking his lips. "I have lots of properties that could use more artwork in them." *And, we have a winner! I'm already halfway to getting into his properties to find the hard drive and I've only just started.*

"I'm not sure how my boss would feel if I started sleeping with my clients. He's all about being professional."

"He doesn't need to know, and you'll only be sleeping with the one," Oliver pointed out. "I'll hire your services personally if there's a problem."

"Now you're making me sound like a prostitute," I glared, crossing my arms over my chest. *Not so smooth anymore, are we, Mr. Kirkham?*

"No, that came out wrong. I'm very sorry, Jade." He was quick to rebuff himself. "I'm just trying to say that I'll do anything to see you again."

"You really want to see me again that badly?"

"Yes," Oliver beamed, shaking his head at me. "Isn't it obvious?"

"I want to see you again, too," I blushed, fidgeting with my napkin.

"Then it's settled! We will see each other again for sure," he grinned. "How about I order some champagne to celebrate?"

"Don't you think that's a little extreme?" I giggled.

"You seem to have that effect on me, Jade," he said with a wink, calling the waiter over.

The meal was wonderful, in part because Oliver spared no expense in spoiling me.

"I think this is the first time I've ever dreaded checking out of a hotel in the morning," Oliver stated on our way back to The Savoy.

"It's been an amazing few days," I yawned as he pulled me against his chest.

He sighed, resting his chin on the top of my head. "It really has. In some ways, I can't believe it's only been two days."

"What time do you leave tomorrow?"

"Lunch time. I have a meeting with the Prime Minister at nine o'clock. I'll leave after that."

"You're meeting the *Prime Minister*?" I gawked, playing up my cover and giving myself more credibility. After all, I shouldn't know that Oliver's company makes weapons or that it was obvious he'd meet with world leaders to discuss any new machines his company was working on.

"I've met him before, Jade," he chuckled, looking down at me. "It's all part of my job considering the company I own. I won't bore you with the details."

"We are worlds apart, Oliver," I sighed as the limo pulled up outside the hotel.

"Not when it comes to the important things," he winked, licking his lips as his eyes roamed my body. He did have a point. When it came to sex, we were equals—compatible in every way.

He just didn't know *how* compatible, yet.

As we stood waiting for the elevator moments later, Oliver made slow, lazy circles on my back with his fingers.

"You look so beautiful in that dress," he whispered, leaning in to kiss my neck. "Please say you're coming up to my room with me."

"Where else would I go?" I smiled, touching his face softly and gasping when I felt my stomach begin to flutter in excitement. I *needed* to control my desire and not allow myself to get too carried away. Oliver seemed to like a more *submissive* Jade. He liked the control, and I would give that to him again tonight. I'd already had my fun with him in the back of the limo earlier, anyway. All I needed to do now was ensure that he was already falling for me so I could begin to dig for information about the hard drive that stored the blueprints.

Oliver's lips were on mine as soon as he closed his bedroom door. His kiss was hungry and desperate as I felt his hands begin to work me out of my dress.

"Fuck, you have no idea how much I want you," he growled, pulling the material down my body. My hands were tangled with his hair as I fought to maintain some control. "I want to be everywhere at once," he whispered hoarsely.

"I'm yours, Oliver. Take me anyway you want." That elicited another snarl from his lips, and he was quick to pick me up by my ass and throw me on his bed.

"I want to taste *this* first," he growled, running his fingers against my covered sex. I arched up to him, which he took as an invitation to slowly pull my panties down my legs. "Would you like that, Jade?" he purred, running his fingers through my slick folds.

"YES!" I moaned, clutching at the pillows behind me. Without another word, Oliver pulled my legs wider apart and began to attack my heated center.

I ground against the rhythm of his tongue. My hands found their way back to his hair, and I gripped it tightly as I thrashed against his glorious torture.

It was difficult to wrap my head around the powers this man had over my body. No man had *ever* been able to make me cum, and well...Oliver could do it in a matter of minutes. I was fully aware of how dangerous that could be for this mission.

He bit down on my clit at the same time he moved his fingers into my dripping wet sex. The motion of his tongue, swirling around my overexcited nerve bundle while his fingers moved frantically in and out of me, pushed me over the edge.

"That's it, Jade. Give in," Oliver mumbled, his lips moving up my body. I almost convulsed when his nose skimmed my hard nipples. His mouth devoured my breasts seconds later, sucking and biting them until I could take no more. "Your body is divine," he muttered when we were finally face to face.

"Is that why you get me naked so quickly?" I giggled, running my hands down his fully clothed body. "Don't you think you should work on your own clothes now?" Oliver bit my neck playfully before he jumped up. I lay on the bed with my arms above my head, waiting and enjoying the show he was putting on. His eyes never stopped roaming my body the entire time he stripped.

"The things I could do to you," he groaned once he joined me back on the bed. Running his hands the entire length of my body first, he then cupped my sex roughly. My eyes rolled to the back of my head and I surrendered to his touch as his fingers slipped inside me once again. "I'm going to fuck you, Jade."

"Ugh...God...yes," I pleaded as his teeth descended onto my nipple and he started pulling and sucking.

"Are you going to let go?"

"Yes," I moaned, moving my hips against his hand while he rubbed my clit.

"Promise me you won't deny yourself anything. I want to feel it all—every last tremor." Christ, Oliver was hot when he spoke this way.

"I promise," I panted wantonly, silently begging for more. My release was so close and I knew it. I could feel myself beginning to build.

"Let go now, and then I'll fuck you," he growled, rubbing my clit faster. I did as he asked and came—*hard*. My entire body jolted, and the most intense orgasm I had ever experienced shot through my limbs, making every nerve ending inside me come to life. Holy hell! If that's what it was like to let go completely, I would definitely do it more often.

"Good girl," Oliver beamed, reaching for a condom and putting it on. "Now, I need you to make sure you do that with my cock inside you."

"I think I can manage that," I panted, wrapping my legs around his waist to draw him closer toward my aching center. I needed him so badly.

"Mm...I like this bolder side of you," he whispered, rotating his hips so the tip of his cock was rubbing against me.

"Please," I moaned, thrusting up toward him.

"What do you want, Jade?"

"You," I gasped. "Please Oliver—fuck me!" A hungry snarl escaped his lips as he thrust into me.

"Tell me to fuck you *hard*!" Oliver's eyes were blazing with a maddening desire. *Oh, someone likes his innocent woman to talk dirty to him. How interesting.*

"Fuck me *hard*, Oliver—now!" I yelled, pushing my hips up toward him. That was all it took for him to lose it. He lifted me up by my ass and began to pound into me at an insane pace. I could hardly contain my gasps, and I was gripping his back so tightly that I knew it was leaving marks.

"Oh...yes! Fuck...Jade," he rambled as he continued to thrust into me hard and fast. His lips traveled between my mouth and my breasts, but when I began to tremble, he slowed his pace. "Not yet, Beautiful, you need to wait for me," he smirked. "I'm almost there." I groaned in frustration, but his lips were soon devouring my breasts again and I forgot I was annoyed. Within minutes, he began to twitch inside me. "Give it all to me, Jade. I need to feel you all over my cock." Shit, I loved Oliver's dirty talk. It was so sexy that I found myself letting go and losing it completely.

Feeling his cock explode inside me as my orgasm washed over me only intensified the high I was riding. Oliver kept me cumming over and over as he trembled above me, releasing everything. Holy shit—*that* was a fucking orgasm!

I was lightheaded when I finally came around.

"Welcome back," he teased, pecking my lips as he gazed down at me.

"Holy shit, Oliver," I panted, clutching my chest as my heart beat wildly. "What the hell was that?"

"A mind-blowing orgasm," he grinned, running his hand down the left side of my body. "That's what can happen when you let it all go."

"Mm...I think I'll be doing that more often," I grinned before succumbing to a yawn. Christ, Oliver had fucked all the energy right out of me.

"Are you tired?"

"A little," I admitted.

"We can sleep now if you want." He had a playful look in his eyes as the words left his lips.

"Really?" I frowned. "You'd give in that easily? You seem a little too sex-crazed for that."

"We can sleep now—I'll just wake you up an hour earlier in the morning and finish having my way with you then," he smoldered, kissing my lips softly before turning his bedside lamp off and pulling me into his arms.

I fell asleep soon after, excited for once to see what the morning would bring.

CHAPTER FOUR

Mmm...I was having the most wonderful dream—one that seemed so real. I could feel myself squirming in my sleep from the vividness of soft lips making their way down my ribs. It wasn't until I felt my legs being moved apart that I realized where I was. *Oh, my! Oliver was clearly a man of his word.*

I opened my eyes the moment I felt his fingers slip into my yearning body.

"Morning, Jade," he smirked as he hovered over me.

"You weren't joking last night about picking up where we left off in the morning, were you?" I giggled. He answered me with a soft kiss, which I returned as he set a slow pace with his fingers.

I'd never really been one for morning sex, because well... truthfully, it wasn't very often that I stayed the entire night. I had to admit, though, that I was looking forward to a few more mornings like this with Oliver.

"I never joke about *this*." Oliver's voice a few moments later was like a trigger that set my orgasm into motion. Before I knew what was happening, I was falling hard and fast. "I don't think I'll ever get enough of watching you come undone, Jade," he smiled once I'd regained myself. As my eyes wandered down his exquisite body, I noticed that he'd already put a condom on.

"We've only known each other for two days. I can't believe how well you know my body already."

"I've never felt this connection with anyone before." Oliver shifted above me and we both groaned as his length pushed against my heated center. "It's going to be hard for me to leave you today. I'm already used to having you around."

"I hope we can meet again soon," I panted, feeling Oliver slowly push deep inside me.

"As soon as I'm free, I'll fly out to you. It will be easier for me to come to you first, " he strained. It only took a second to let go, and when I did, I became a slave to his touches.

❋ ❋ ❋

"You're eating breakfast?" he questioned over the table a few hours later. I could now happily admit that I *loved* morning sex! It was clearly the *best* way to start any day.

"Well, it *is* the most important meal of the day," I grinned, taking a bite of my toast. "Not to mention, I think I need the energy after my early morning wake-up call."

"I'm impressed," Oliver chuckled, continuing to read his newspaper.

"Are you nervous about your meeting this morning?" I asked, pouring myself some more coffee.

"No. I'm used to these kinds of meetings." He didn't even look up from the article in front of him as he spoke.

"Have you met many world leaders in the past?"

"I've met most of them, actually." His tone was a little

arrogant as he looked up to smirk at me. *Oh, Oliver... You have no idea, but I already know every little detail about you.*

"You've met *most* of them?" I gawked with my mouth hanging open. Yeah, I had this act down to a fine art. "Jesus, Oliver, if these are the people you socialize with, what the hell are you doing with me?"

"It's my job, Jade. I don't *choose* to socialize with them. Trust me, I'd much rather spend the rest of the day with you." He had a gleam in his eyes as he spoke, and I only needed one guess as to what was crossing his mind at the moment. I decided to play with him a bit.

"Is everything about sex with you?" I asked innocently, running my hands through my hair and tilting my head slightly to expose more of my neck to him. I was wearing one of his shirts, and only a few buttons were buttoned.

"What do you mean by that?" By his tone, I thought I might have offended him.

"I was just wondering if that's what *this* is." I started fidgeting with my napkin, intently focused on the task instead of on Oliver. Innocent girls avoided eye contact when it was a conversation that mattered to them, and I needed to know how far I'd gotten with him this weekend. I only had six months to secure the blueprints, and that wasn't very long if I didn't get to see him every week.

"Jade, I really have no idea. All I know is that I am deeply attracted to you. Isn't that enough for now?" I looked up into his burning, dark eyes. *Christ, a woman could drown in pure desire from those scorching orbs.*

"I'm sorry. I'll stop with the heavy," I conceded, looking at my watch. "What time are you leaving?"

"In about ten minutes," he sighed deeply, raking his eyes over me. "I don't even have time to take you again."

I choked a little on my coffee, nearly spitting it across the table. "Wasn't the five times earlier enough?" Oh, this guy had stamina; I had to give him that. Oliver would be like my dream man if I actually had the option to date. *Why did he have to be my target? Why couldn't I have met him after my contract ended?*

"No," he smoldered, getting up from his chair. *He cannot be serious!*

"You're meeting the Prime Minister, remember?" I pointed out as he pulled me out of my chair and to my feet. "I'm pretty sure he's not the kind of guy who likes tardiness."

"I'll be counting each day until I can see you again," Oliver said with a sigh as he ran his nose down my neck. I couldn't help but arch up toward him as his hand gripped my ass firmly. "Oh, the things I'm going to do to you when I see you again, Jade. Maybe it's a good thing we'll be apart for a few weeks."

"You mean there's more?"

I groaned as his left hand moved to palm my breasts over his shirt.

"I haven't even started with you yet, Beautiful," he murmured huskily before his lips crashed against mine.

I was breathless when we finally broke apart. "You'll call me as soon as you arrive home, won't you?" I pleaded, running my hands over the back collar of his shirt.

"Yes," Oliver smiled, caressing my face softly. "Okay, now I really need to leave." He seemed honestly troubled by that, as if he didn't want to go. Wow, I never thought it would be this easy. Then again, I did still have the task of finding out which property stored his secure hard drive. That wasn't going to be easy.

"Enjoy your meeting," I grinned, "and tell the Prime Minister I said 'Hi.'" Oliver chuckled as he kissed me softly, his hands lingering on my face before he pulled away.

"I'm really glad I met you, Jade Gibbs. I will see you *very* soon."

"I'm looking forward to it," I blushed, watching his eyes roam over me one last time before he turned to leave.

"You're welcome to get ready here. Just let reception know once you've checked out," he called over his shoulder, picking up his briefcase. His luggage had already been taken down earlier when the breakfast cart had been delivered.

"Okay, thank you," I replied, smiling weakly.

"I'll call you every day if you want me to." Oliver appeared to be stalling, and I was pretty sure I knew why. *Jade, you have well and truly hooked him.*

"Only if you have the time," I answered, playing with my hands.

"I'll *make* the time." His voice was firm as he took one last look at me and then finally left.

Wow, this mission was going effortlessly so far.

* * *

"It's good to have you back, Jade," Sonia said as she smiled at me from behind her desk. "How did the first contact go?"

"I've made arrangements to meet the target again in two weeks. He's coming to Florida to see me."

"He's traveling to *you*?" she gasped. "How do you do it? I've never known a Seductor as capable as you before."

"I just use my charm," I winked as she passed me more paperwork that had to do with Oliver.

"These are the nine properties Mr. Kirkham owns. It appears he rents a few out to close family and friends, so that refines the search a little."

I glanced through the paperwork and noticed Oliver had a family home in Macon, Georgia. That wasn't too far away from where I lived at Headquarters in St. Petersburg, Florida, and I wondered how often he stayed there. That could be extremely useful in the months ahead.

"Do you think you'll have time for a few side jobs?" Sonia questioned, getting up to pour us both a cup of coffee.

"As long as they don't interfere with this mission, I can't see why not."

"I might need you and Molly for a small assignment next week."

"Just let me know," I replied, still reading the files in front of me. Oliver had properties in Macon, Dubai, London, Italy, New York, and Canada. It was going to be difficult trying to persuade him to take me to each of them without him getting suspicious, but I knew I could manage it if I played my cards right.

"I think that's everything. Oh, Mario has the keys to the apartment. He moved out last night." I was excited that I was getting the penthouse since I'd never been on a mission large enough to be granted that perk, but why did I have to pick up the keys from *Mario*?

Mario was the top male Seductor, and had just finished a mission that was worth over three million dollars. I only knew this because I helped with it at the beginning, playing the ex-girlfriend whose heart he broke. The cover story was perfect—if his target came knocking, I would say he left me the penthouse as an apology for what he had done.

Mario was sunbathing by the pool when I found him. He'd earned the nickname *Mr. Vain* for a reason.

"Still working on that tan, Mario?" I teased, squirting some tanning lotion at him.

"Hey, watch it," he grumbled, jumping up quickly. "I have to show these pecks off in the best way that I can." Mario did have an amazing body, but he was a *Seductor,* after all. We *had* to be perfect; it was one of the many *rules*.

"I need the keys to the penthouse," I sighed, crossing my arms.

"Then you'll need to frisk me for them, Jade," he winked, licking his lips. It wasn't uncommon for Seductors to 'get it on' from time to time as long as it didn't get serious—our founder wasn't against that—but Mario was quite possibly the biggest dickhead in the Seductors, with Alicia coming in a close second. She was an exotic beauty with tanned skin, long black hair, and deep brown eyes, but her looks were really the only thing she had going for her. Alicia and Mario's egos were big enough for all the Seductors that they currently had on contract. Mario actually thought no one could resist him, and that was the biggest turnoff in my eyes. Yes, we were *Seductors*, but we weren't *Gods*.

"Well, that wouldn't take long. You're not packing much down there, Mario," I quipped, looking down at his small swim trunks. I noticed the apartment keys were on top of the book he'd been reading, so I was stretching to pick them up when Mario suddenly grabbed me around my waist.

"Why do you deny me, Jade? We could be so good together. You know it isn't the size of the tool, anyway. It's how you use it," he whispered huskily, running his hand down my back. I was fucking livid. Would the asshole ever get the hint? I wasn't easy like Alicia was; she was practically stuck to his dick whenever they were both at headquarters.

I turned, hitting him hard in the nuts with my knee before pulling his arm tight behind his back and making him cry out in agony.

"Sorry, Mario, but truthfully, you're just not my type. Besides, I wouldn't touch anything that Alicia has been around with a ten-foot pole," I spat, stretching for the keys before I let him fall to the ground in pain. The few Seductors around the pool chuckled softly as I stormed off.

"Whoa, what's bugging you?" Molly asked as I charged into our room.

"Fucking Mario!" I seethed.

"What has he done now?"

"He's such a fucking jerk! Molly, why did you sleep with him?"

"He's a good fuck, what can I say?" she shrugged. "You should give it a go. I..."

"No, I'm good, thanks. I'm not really one for sharing. Anyway, I'm just glad Georgie never succumbed to his powers too," I interrupted as I began to pack my things.

"Are you leaving tonight?" Molly sulked, lying on my bed.

"Yeah, I need to get everything ready. My target is meeting me in two weeks, and the apartment is an empty shell right now. I need to make it look lived in."

"I can't believe you got the penthouse. What's your target like? Is he hot?" Molly and her goddamn questions—she knew the rules. *When was Georgie getting back again? Surely her mission was nearly complete.*

"He is very pleasing to the eyes."

"Is he good in bed?"

Christ, *good* didn't even begin to cover it. "He's not *too* bad." I smiled slyly over at her, and by the look in her eyes, I could tell she saw right through me. She was about to say something when my Seductor cell phone rang. It could only be one person.

"Speaking of lover boy..." Molly giggled, throwing my phone at me. "I'll give you some privacy." With a wink, she turned to leave.

"Hi," I breathed, answering on the third ring.

"Hi, Beautiful," Oliver replied with a sigh. "You sound out of breath. What have you been doing?"

"I had to run to my phone. I was on the other side of my apartment." Fucking Mario and his wandering hands. I was still angry and needed to calm down.

"Wow, how big is this apartment?" Shit, I actually had no idea.

"It's big enough," I giggled.

"Are you sure you don't mind me staying with you when I come down? I can book a hotel instead, if it's easier."

"I want you here, Oliver," I replied immediately and without an ounce of doubt. The truth was, I couldn't wait to see him again. It had only been three days since we'd parted, but my body was already craving his touches. "How is work?"

"Boring. All I can think about is you. I kept writing your name over and over again on a scrap piece of paper, even."

"Wow! You sound like you have it bad," I giggled.

"I think I do," he exhaled.

"Do we really have to wait another eleven days?"

"If I seal this deal before then, I'll call you. It's all looking promising, but it could still fall through. Richard is working hard."

"Richard?"

"He's my lawyer and uncle, actually."

"Wow! So it's a family business, then?" I questioned. I'd need to be careful about that. I didn't want any of his family members to be wary of my intentions toward him, after all. He was a wealthy man, and many beautiful women may have already tried to charm him to gain his wealth.

"There aren't many of us Kirkham's left. We have to stick together." Did I detect some sorrow in his voice? "I need to go, Jade. I'm needed in a meeting."

"Go. It's fine."

"I just wanted to let you know that I can't wait to see you again."

"I can't wait, either." I was actually smiling when I said it because of how true the words were. What the hell was up with that? Oliver couldn't even see me.

"Bye, Jade."

"Bye, Oliver."

With that, I hung up and finished packing, excited to move into my penthouse apartment. I really couldn't wait to get away from headquarters for a while. Well, that's what I kept telling myself, anyway. Deep down, I worried it had more to do with seeing Oliver again than anything else.

This was a mission; I could *not* get attached.

❋ ❋ ❋

"You need to focus," Molly grinned while I hit the punching bag. We had fitness training in an hour and were warming up.

"I *am* focused," I complained. "Why would you think I wasn't?"

"You usually hit the bag with more force, that's all."

"Do you think you'll pass the fitness test?" I asked,

changing the subject. Molly hated fitness, but it was a large part of being a Seductor. We had to keep our bodies beautiful and all that crap.

"I'm not sure. Oh, I hope they don't make me give up chocolate again." I tried to hide my giggle at that. Jason, our fitness coach, always took away our favorite food if we failed his tests. It was one way to keep us motivated. Being in charge of our physical fitness wasn't his only job in the Seductors. He was one of our four hit men, too. If a mission failed, one or more of our hit men would collect the steal—no matter the price. Often it meant the life of the target. They'd make it look like an accident, of course, or a burglary gone wrong. Nothing was ever left to chance.

"It will be your own fault if he does," I sniggered at Molly.

"You haven't spoken much about your new mission since you got back," she mused a while later.

"There isn't much to tell. It was only a first encounter."

"But you slept with him. Jade, you hardly ever sleep with a target on a first meet."

"I don't always see the need to use sex in every mission. We are given other skills to use, too."

"But sex is always the skill that gains a steal no matter what. Don't you pay attention in training?"

"I think you've interpreted it wrong," I sighed, shaking my head. Molly frowned at me. "Seduction isn't just about getting someone into your bed. You can control a stranger *long* before that. A soft touch, a suggestive sentence. It's all about gaining that person's trust, making them believe you want them. Once you have that, the steal is easy."

"But I enjoy the sex," Molly complained, sulking like a

petulant child.

"Why do I even bother?" I sighed, noticing it was time for our fitness test. "I'd eat a chocolate bar while you can. It's time for our test," I teased.

"Bitch," Molly muttered under her breath.

I giggled, grabbing my towel to wipe the sweat from my forehead as we walked to the gym. "Maybe, but you still love me!"

✻ ✻ ✻

"I hate the fucking bleep test," Molly moaned before we'd even started. "What's the point of sprinting back and forth, anyway? Just to beat the damn buzzer?"

"Does she ever shut up?" Zara asked with a smirk, stretching her arms and legs to loosen up.

"No," I winked, watching Molly glare at me.

There were five other Seductors here today. Allie and Oscar were fairly new recruits like Zara. They had just completed their first year. Oscar was our weapons expert—he'd come straight from the military. Allie, on the other hand, almost joined Intelligence instead of becoming a seductor. She was our best hacker, but decided she loved the *thrill* the missions brought her.

Jack joined around the same time as me and was a bit of a loner. He did everything he could to avoid crowds and keep to himself. He was a people watcher, though, and an expert in body language.

Most Seductors had their own unique skills, on top of the ones we trained for. It made us stronger as a unit and also helped Sonia decide which of us to assign to each case.

My unique skill was one that Sonia valued the most, and was the reason she classified me as her top Seductor. I could seduce anyone with my words and body language. If I chose to take them to bed, they were mine for life. I could get anything out of them I wanted, and sometimes all it took was the right seductive look or the perfect sway to my hips as I walked.

Mario was in the far corner of the gym, stretching with his partner in crime, Alicia. Those two made my skin boil. They were a deadly duo, though. Alicia had skills very similar to mine. She liked to think she was better than me, but she wasn't. Mario, however, was a trained assassin. Molly and Georgie often told me I needed to be careful around him because of what he could do, but assassin or not, he didn't scare me.

"Right!" Jason clapped his hands together. "I hope you've all kept your fitness levels up this month. I want each of you to beat your personal best today."

"Great," Molly muttered. "There goes my chocolate bars for the month." I tried to hide my snigger but apparently failed. "Yeah, laugh it up, Miss Fit."

"You'll be fine." I rolled my eyes as the first beep sounded.

I found the bleep test easy because I'd always loved running. It gave me a sense of freedom—a way to clear my head.

"Keep up the pace, people. You shouldn't be feeling the burn yet," Jason shouted toward us. "Molly, move those legs faster!" *Poor Molly.* She might just be right about losing her right to eat chocolate for a month.

"You've lost your edge, Jade," Alicia sneered while we stretched out after our test. Molly had been lucky this time; actually, we had all passed.

"Only by a few seconds," I glared. "I still beat *your* best time."

"Whatever," she muttered, sipping her water and walking off.

"You two don't get along, do you?" Zara questioned.

"Is it that obvious?" I snorted.

"A little, yeah," she replied, clearly waiting for me to explain why.

"We just clash at times, that's all."

"Is that because you're so similar?" Alicia and me *similar*? I would probably start to dislike Zara if she kept talking like that.

"Who knows," I shrugged, looking at the time. I needed to start getting the penthouse ready soon.

"You did well today, Jade," Jason commented, walking out of the gym with me. "I'm going for a long distance run later if you wanted to join me."

"I would, but I need to get ready for my mission."

"Oh, yeah. I've heard about this *top* mission." Seriously, the gossip was worse here than it had ever been in high school.

"Not you, too," I sighed. "Why does Sonia insist on all these rules if everyone breaks them?"

"You know we can talk about the basics. We just aren't allowed to go into full detail. Is it as huge as everyone is saying?"

"I'd say that's talking about details, Jas," I giggled, walking into my room. "Enjoy your run." With a grin, I closed my door.

CHAPTER FIVE

The penthouse had left me awestruck when I first arrived. It was a truly beautiful place, with a full panoramic view of St. Pete Beach and the marina. The apartment itself was very modern and was awash with pristine, white walls, so I'd already spent the better part of last week looking for interesting pieces of artwork to put up to add a little bit of color to the place. Plus, I had to ensure the apartment looked like the home of an art lover; Oliver thought that was my job, after all. Not to mention, I had filled the space with little pieces of myself—from old CDs that I could never quite part with, to books I read so much the spines were falling apart, and fake photos of me with friends. I say *fake*, but the pictures of Georgie and me in China were real. I couldn't chance the photos of Molly and me, knowing that she would be helping me out on this mission.

I had officially fallen in love with my bedroom—well, mainly my bed. It was a large four-poster bed, but the frame and posts were set in steel that was interwoven, almost like enchanted branches from a fairy tale. The posts—straight at the bottom but curved inward at the top—joined together to create a small arch on the top of the bed. I'd bought some rich red fabric to drape over the frame, and I had to admit, it looked like a cozy little love nest now. All I needed was for Oliver to arrive and it would be complete.

Having kept to his word, Oliver called me almost every day since we'd been apart. The plan was for him to stay with me for three days before he had to return to New York for an important business meeting at the end of the week.

I had told him that I'd managed to get the same three days off from work, but that I might need to go into the office one afternoon just to touch base with the receptionist, who was being played by Molly. Sonia had already set up the fake 'Denning's Interior Design' headquarters in an office building downtown, so I'd be able to take Oliver to my 'place of work' if I needed to.

I'd just been food shopping and was starting to put everything away when my intercom rang. Glancing at the clock, I realized that Oliver wasn't due for another few hours. Surely it couldn't be him already, could it?

"I have a delivery for a Miss Gibbs," a voice said over the intercom.

"Oh, okay," I replied, pushing the button to let him into the lobby area of the building. A few moments later, I opened the door to a bouquet of deep red roses. Once I'd signed for them, I shut the door and checked the note. Oliver. *My, he really is a charmer.*

These aren't as beautiful as you, Jade, but I wanted to send you something.

I can't wait to see you, which will be in a few hours by the time you receive these.

Oliver

xxxxxx

Smiling to myself, I put the roses in some water, unable to remember the last time anyone had brought me flowers.

All I had left to do was get myself ready, so once the groceries were put away, I made my way into my bathroom to have a nice long soak in the bathtub. Something told me I would need to relax my body for Oliver's onslaught when he arrived in a few hours.

Keeping my makeup to a minimum when I finished my bath, I then blow-dried my hair loosely and put on a pair of denim shorts and a pale pink T-shirt. Once I was ready, I decided to read a book and sit on my balcony until Oliver arrived. I had offered to pick him up from the airport, but he'd insisted on finding his own way. It wasn't very often I got to drive my pale blue Mercedes Benz E Class Convertible, but I guess that would have to wait for another day. I was definitely going to take him out for a tour around the town while he was here. That was all part of my innocent Jade character.

I hadn't been sitting for long when my intercom rang. *Showtime!*

"Hello?" I asked.

"Hi, Beautiful," Oliver sighed over the intercom. Damn, just his voice was making me wet. I *had* to get that under control. "Are you going to let me up?"

"Sure," I replied, pushing the button to let him in. "I'm in the penthouse."

"Okay."

Like a giddy school girl, I waited for the knock at the door. I pretended it was because I was getting back into character, but the truth was, a small part of me couldn't wait to see him again.

Finally, the knock came and I opened the door to a very casual looking Oliver in faded blue jeans and a crisp, white linen shirt. He was a *seriously* good looking guy. I also noticed he was holding a single red rose. *More flowers?*

"Isn't that supposed to be in your mouth or something?" I giggled, motioning toward the rose as Oliver stood there in all his perfection.

"I wouldn't be able to do this if that was the case," he beamed, pulling me toward him and crashing his lips against mine. I gasped into his mouth, my hands molding themselves to his back as his tongue began to caress mine. *Christ, he tasted good.*

"Now *that's* what I call a kiss hello," he winked when we broke apart.

"Thank you for the roses—you really shouldn't have," I smiled, taking the single rose from his hand as I let him into the apartment.

"Wow, this is a nice place you have, Jade," Oliver mused, his eyes darting everywhere at once. I noticed he'd only brought one large suitcase with him, and figured he might as well take in straight to my bedroom. *Good plan, Jade—get Oliver into the bedroom right away.*

"Did you want to put your bag down? You can put it in my bedroom if you want."

Oliver's eyes darkened and he shook his head at me. "Trying to get me into your bedroom the moment I walk through your door? Jade, I thought you were a sweet, innocent young woman."

"I was trying to be practical," I lied, forcing a blush.

"Which door is it?"

"I'll show you," I offered with a shy smile, walking down the hallway to my room.

I could feel Oliver close behind me, and I knew the shorts I was wearing were probably driving him crazy. They didn't leave much to the imagination.

"So, this is it," I muttered as we walked in.

"Wow, that's a bed," Oliver gasped, setting his suitcase down.

"Yeah, I fell in love with the frame," I explained with my back to him. I could feel the heat radiating off his body as he drew closer toward me.

"It's very mystical. Almost like a bed from a fairy tale," he muttered against my neck.

"Does that make you my knight in shining armor?"

"I can be if you need saving," he whispered, stroking my neck with the back of his hand. I groaned at his touch, having been starved of it for too long. "I've missed you so much, Jade." His hands wrapped around my waist from behind as he spoke. "I've missed the feel of your skin." He ran his fingertips over my arms lightly. "But do you know what I've missed the most?" he asked, spinning me around to face him. I shook my head, completely spellbound by his words. "I've missed your soft whimpers when you come undone at my hands." I held back a groan as I felt Oliver undo the button of my shorts.

"Jade, did you miss me?"

"Yes," I panted as he backed me toward the bed.

"This bed is giving me some very strong visual images," he smirked, pulling my shorts down my body before moving to remove my T-shirt. Gently, Oliver pushed me down onto the bed.

"Now tell me, Jade, have you been thinking of me in this bed?" he purred as his hands slipped between my legs and ran over my panties.

"A woman never tells that secret," I murmured, feeling his fingers start to make small circles against my sex.

"I think you did," he groaned. "I think you've brought yourself to the brink several times over these last two weeks, wishing your fingers were mine."

"Ugh," I thrusted up toward his hand as he put a little more pressure on my sex. I wanted his fingers inside me, damnit!

"Tell me, Jade. I want to know."

"Yes," I panted. "Yes...I made myself cum thinking of you." How was he doing this to me?

"Mm..." he hummed as his hands finally slipped inside my panties. "How did you make yourself cum? Did you play with this?" Oliver's fingers began to rub my clit up and down, and I was so turned on that I was beginning to tremble. "Or maybe you did it like this." Every muscle in my body constricted as he slipped two fingers inside me and began a slow, torturous pace. "Which way was it, Jade? Tell me or I'll stop."

"Ugh...ugh...it was both ways," I strained. "Oh, God... Oliver." I could feel myself building already, and I had no idea how that was even possible.

"Shit, that's a hot thought—you, naked in this bed and touching yourself. I would've loved to have watched." His words were going to make me combust! No, scratch that...they were going to make me cum.

I came loudly, trembling in a pure state of bliss.

"Wow," I gasped when I finally opened my eyes. "You're fully clothed *again.* One of these days I am going to strip you naked first."

"Is that a promise?" Oliver smiled lazily as I sat up and started to unbutton his shirt.

"Maybe," I grinned, pushing it down his shoulders and then off his back. Christ, he had an incredible body—toned in all the right places.

"You're not naked yet, anyway," he commented, playing with the straps of my bra. "You have great taste in underwear, Jade." I had a feeling he would like my blue frilly underwear if he were to see it. "But as sexy as you look in them, they have to go."

"Can't I at least take your jeans off first?" I pouted.

"A little eager, are we?" he winked, licking his lips.

I blushed, looking away from him. "Is it that obvious?"

"Hey, don't feel guilty about wanting me, Jade. I can't even begin to explain the desire I have for you. I want to be everywhere at once, but I also don't want to rush this." I closed my eyes as I felt his hands sweep around my neck before caressing my face. "You make me hum with a need I've never felt before. A desire that I can feel in every cell of my body."

"Wow!" I gasped, moving my hand to stroke his face. "That's how I feel every time you touch me." I couldn't read the expression on Oliver's face, but he knocked me breathless with his kiss as he pushed me back down onto the bed, his hands were quick to pull my bra cups down. He kissed his way down my neck, and when his lips made contact with my yearning nipples, jolts of pleasure shot through my body like bolts of lightning.

"Oliver, I need more," I begged, rubbing my drenched, panty covered sex against his leg.

"A little impatient, aren't we?" he chuckled against my left breast, taking a long, slow lick against my nipple before sucking it into his mouth.

"Oh, fuck...please!" Was this what it felt like for all the men I had seduced over the years? To be at the mercy of someone who could control your body with the simplest touch? Oliver *wasn't* a Seductor, though. He hadn't been taught how to give someone pleasure to gain what you needed. He was doing this because he *wanted* me to come undone by his touch alone. That scared me, but what frightened me more was the fact that I was willingly letting him do it.

"You're doing it again, Jade," he grumbled against my ear. "Stop fighting it." I arched back as he thrust two fingers into my waiting center. "Why do you deny what your body wants? You can't stop it from happening. If I feel you denying yourself, I'll just work that much harder." I fisted my hands into the sheets as Oliver's pace became so frantic that I could hardly keep my eyes open. "Give it up, Jade. I mean it!" Shit! His words were my undoing and I fell for a second time in a matter of minutes.

With hardly any time to regain my senses, Oliver was ripping my panties from my body. I heard the familiar foil wrapper sound, and when I opened my eyes, he was gloriously naked above me.

"Don't you *dare* fight this," he warned, thrusting deep inside me. Oh, it was heaven to be this full. He lifted my legs, wrapping them around his waist before slamming into me again.

"Fuck...yes," I moaned.

"Do you want this, Jade?"

What a stupid question. "YES!"

"If I feel you fighting it, I'll stop. I mean it," he glared, groaning as he rotated his hips. I knew he could feel how wet I was for him.

"I won't fight it," I whimpered, lifting myself up to capture his lips with my own as I clawed at his back. "I want you, Oliver. Fuck me!" A growl escaped him before he thrust deeper inside me. Fuck, I was sure he had just hit my G spot. *I didn't even think I had one of those.* "Holy fuck," I yelled, throwing my hands over my face and trying to keep some form of control. As Oliver hit *that* spot over and over again, I realized I was losing the battle. I couldn't make sense of *anything.* Hell, I couldn't even remember my full name.

"Oh, I think I've just found what I've been looking for," he smirked, rolling his hips and grabbing my ass to push deeper inside. Shit, he hit it *again.*

"Oliver...Oliver...Oh, Oliver!" I kept chanting his name as I began to build again. My hands were in his sweaty hair now, and I was clinging to him so tightly I was worried I might be hurting him. He didn't seem to care, though; he was too focused on his rhythm as he fucked me.

The pressure growing inside me was going to lift me into another dimension when it exploded, and all I had to hold me to this earth was Oliver. I clung to him tightly, and with one more thrust against *that* spot, I fell. There was no fear—I knew that wherever I landed, Oliver would catch me.

I could get used to these kinds of orgasms.

❊ ❊ ❊

"Welcome back," he grinned down at me. I had no idea how long I'd been out for.

"Jesus, Oliver," I gasped. "What the hell are you *doing* to me?"

"I'm making your body come alive, Beautiful," he purred, kissing my lips softly. "But before I do that again, can I get a drink and something to eat? I'm starving."

Thank Christ for that! I actually needed to rest myself.

I made Oliver and myself a quick chicken stir-fry while he glanced around my apartment, taking everything in. I wasn't worried; I knew I had filled it with enough evidence to make it look as if I'd lived here for a while.

"You have a great place here," he smiled. "Is it yours or are you renting?"

"Renting," I replied. "I'm not sure if I'm ready to settle down just yet. You never know what the future holds."

"That's very true," he called, studying one of the paintings I'd purchased last week. "I love this painting, Jade." It was a painting of a harbor sunrise at a beautiful spot not too far from the marina. I loved the artist's use of color, which was why I bought it. Actually, I had enjoyed looking around *all* the local art studios. It gave me a chance to get my name out there to help with my cover story while Oliver was here. "I have a thing about harbors, too. Well, paintings of harbors, that is."

"Really?" *We have something in common.* I smiled over at him, his body was quite distracting. He was only wearing his sweats, leaving his well toned chest on full display. Talk about washboard abs—I wanted to run my tongue up and down every inch of them. "The *Harbor Sunrise* is a favorite local painting of mine. The artist lives nearby. I can take you to his workshop while you're here, if you want. You might see a few pieces you like."

"I'd like that." Oliver turned his full attention back to

me. "I'll have to show you the few paintings that I own at my properties."

"I thought you needed my services. If you already have paintings, there isn't much for me to do," I teased, dishing up the food.

"I don't have many, but I have a few valuable pieces I'd love to show you." He took a seat at the table he'd already set earlier. I couldn't believe how excited he sounded about taking me to his home. *Oh, Oliver, if only you knew the truth. You'll fall right into the trap.*

"Are you asking me to stay at your place?" I giggled, placing his food down in front of him.

"I'm asking you to be at one of them," he grinned.

"You have more than one?" I gasped, acting shocked. "Actually, why am I not surprised?"

"What do you mean?"

"You have your own company. Of course you'd own a few properties," I muttered, playing with my food.

"I don't just have a few, Jade. I have nine." I choked on a mouthful of stir-fry so Oliver passed me my glass of water. "Does that bother you? I mean, to know I'm *that* rich?" he asked in concern.

I shook my head. "It doesn't bother me, but I'm finding it hard to understand what you're doing here with me, Oliver."

"There's something about you, Jade. I can't put my finger on it yet, but you captivate me."

"I'm just an average, working woman. I'm nothing special," I sighed, using my poor little Jade approach.

"You can't see it, can you?" he smiled, stroking my face.

I frowned. "See what?"

He seemed lost in thought as he gazed at me for a few short moments, and then something crossed his mind. I could see him trying to shake the thought away before he finally spoke. "You can't see what an amazing cook you are. This is incredible," he chuckled, playing off the intense conversation we had clearly just had.

It made me wonder what Oliver had really been thinking about before.

It was safe to say that I was well and truly on my way to gaining those blueprints, so why did my heart feel heavy at the thought of completing this mission?

CHAPTER SIX

Oliver was completely carefree when he wasn't working. We didn't even get out of bed until mid-afternoon on our first full day together—not that I was complaining. He *definitely* knew how to fill the time.

I was taking him out for some seafood near the marina tonight, and was planning on pretending to get drunk so I could have some fun with him. I wasn't used to being so subdued in the bedroom, and Oliver had a body to *die* for. I couldn't wait to get my expert hands on him later when I could chalk it up to the alcohol making me bolder.

"I might look into renting my own property around here," Oliver mused as we sat on my balcony, watching the Marina in the distance.

"What would be the point?" I frowned. "You'd be staying with me anyway."

"Oh, I would, would I?" Oliver grinned, moving a little closer to me. We'd only been out of bed for an hour or so, yet my body was already yearning for more. "A little smitten, are we, Jade?"

"I thought that was obvious the night we met," I giggled, tucking my hair behind my ears, trying to act a little uncomfortable.

"I never like to presume anything," he smiled, slowly letting his gaze wander down my legs. I smiled shyly, my eyes focused on my watch.

"We need to think about getting ready soon. It's getting late," I said as I stretched and stood up.

"Mm..." Oliver groaned, pulling me down onto his lap. "Would you like me to wash your back in the shower? I give amazing massages."

"Is there anything you can't do?" I sniggered, bracing myself by gripping his strong shoulders tightly.

"I can't sing," he teased before leaning up to capture my lips with his. It was only a chaste kiss and I was glad. I really did need to get ready.

Chuckling, I pushed off his shoulders as he let me go. "Somehow, I don't believe you."

"No, really—I'm tone-deaf when it comes to singing."

"Maybe I *should* let you come shower with me then so I can see if you're telling me the truth or not," I winked.

"That can be arranged if you want, although, I can't promise I'll even sing in the shower. I might be too busy with something else." Did I really want to know what Oliver would be too busy doing? *Yes, of course I did.*

"Busy doing what?" I purred as he stood up, watching me with hungry eyes.

"You really want me to spell it out, Jade?" he muttered huskily, running his hand down my back before cupping my ass. I nodded, closing my eyes for a short second while I tried to regain myself. Was I really acting when it came to these feelings? I wasn't so sure anymore; they seemed a little *too* real to me. "You know I won't have time to sing while I'm fucking you hard with my fingers against your shower wall, Jade," he continued.

"Fuck, Oliver," I groaned, more than turned on by his dirty words as he pulled me toward him.

"I love it when you swear, Beautiful. It's so unlike you, and I know it's because I've got you all worked up." Oliver began to undo the buttons on my shorts as he spoke. "So, how about that shower, then?" I couldn't resist this guy. What the hell was wrong with me? "I take it from your panting, that's a yes?" he chuckled, taking my hand and leading me to the bathroom. What was happening to me? I was quickly becoming addicted to the powers this guy held over my body.

He stripped first the moment we were in the bathroom. Damn, I could look at his body all day. Why did he want the shy, subdued Jade? Oh, the things I could do to this man if he would just let me be wild.

"Your turn," Oliver winked, stalking over to me. I was so mesmerized by his impressive member—standing tall, proud, and *so* ready for me—that I hardly felt him strip me of my clothes. Well, until he pinched my nipples between his fingers, that is. "I think it's time to get you nice and *wet*, Jade." His hands glided down toward my sex. "Mm..." he cooed, inserting two fingers, "it seems we're already halfway there."

"Oliver," I gasped. "Jesus, do you *ever* stop?"

"Not with you, it would seem." He removed his hand, only to bring it up to his mouth, tasting me. "Why don't you turn the water on?" he muttered, sucking on his fingers. Oh, God, I was going to combust if he kept doing that.

I stepped into the shower and turned the water on, groaning as Oliver pushed me against the cold tiles.

"You do know a shower is all about foreplay, don't you?" he snarled, biting down on my earlobe. "Sex in a shower is very dangerous."

"Is that so?" I panted. "I've always liked the idea of sex in the shower." I played along, leaning against the wall as he snaked his hands around me to grab my breasts firmly from behind.

"Oh, I'm sure we could have a lot of fun in this shower," he said huskily as I felt him grind his erection against my ass, sending chills up my spine.

"Mm…I think you could be right."

"But I can assure you, I *won't* be singing," he purred, moving one hand down toward my sex while the other worked my nipples, pulling and rolling his thumb over each one and making me arch back toward him. "I love it when you let go, Jade. I can feel you giving your body over to me." I palmed the wall as Oliver thrust his fingers deep inside me, hitting *that* spot instantly. I worried that my legs might collapse beneath me once he had helped me reach my peak, but my fear melted away when he wrapped one arm around my waist and held me up as he set a maddening pace with his other hand.

"Give it to me, Jade. I'm not going to stop until you let go." Christ, he was so controlling but I loved it. For the first time since I'd become a Seductor, I could really let go. Oliver knew how to work my body unlike any man I'd ever known. "That's it, Beautiful," he cooed as I fell apart in his arms. The hot water from the shower trickled down both our bodies as we moved farther under the showerhead. It was beyond erotic, and I'd had some *great* sexual experiences so far in my lifetime.

I couldn't resist stretching out behind me to run my hands through his wet hair while I came back down from my high.

"Mm...Oh...Oliver," I groaned out as he pulled my nipples with his forefingers and thumbs.

"I could play with your body all day," he said as he bit down on my neck, nipping me playfully. All I wanted to do was reach behind me and stroke his erection that was pressing into my ass cheeks, but I knew shy Jade wouldn't react that way.

"We don't have time for that," I panted, moving him even farther under the jets with me. "I thought you wanted me to take you out?"

"I think we have time for some lovemaking, too."

"We could do that later," I complained, closing my eyes as he began to wash me.

"You're right. I imagine you might be a little sore down here." As Oliver spoke, he ran the washcloth between my legs. *Oh, it felt so good.*

"Well, we *have* been a little busy since the moment you arrived."

Oliver sighed deeply in my ear before turning me to face him. "What are you doing to me, Jade Gibbs?" He looked conflicted and so damn beautiful. With his hair soaking wet and beaten down from the water, it looked almost black.

"What do you mean?" I frowned as he began to gently wash my shoulders.

"I've never been so physically attracted to anyone before. It's scaring the shit out of me because I don't know how to control it. I can't keep my hands off you."

"Then *don't* control it," I whispered, wrapping my arms around his neck. It didn't matter that he was affecting me physically, too, because I had a job to do. I had to make him fall for me so he would trust me. "Just feel it, Oliver," I pleaded. "I'm scared, too."

"Jade, I know nothing about you. You have to understand why I'm nervous."

"There is hardly anything to know about me." I smiled as I felt his hands cup my ass, bringing me flush against his body.

"I doubt that, Jade. I can feel there is something deeper inside you, and I can't wait to find out what that is." *Oh, Oliver. You might regret saying that one day.*

"Good luck trying to find it. I think you might be wrong. I'm just plain, boring, Jade," I giggled.

"You are anything but plain, Beautiful," he murmured, leaning down to capture my lips. Soon, we were lost as we began to explore each other's bodies, washing and massaging until we were both fully satisfied.

* * *

I took Oliver to one of my favorite seafood places—*The Oyster Bar*—once we were finally ready. It was only a short walk from the penthouse, yet I was surprised that he held my hand the entire way.

I had decided to go for a casual, blue linen dress that was still tight enough to tempt him with my sexy figure and strappy black sandals.

"This is amazing," Oliver mumbled through a mouthful of lobster.

"This place does have the best seafood in town," I grinned, sipping my beer.

"And what a view," he commented toward the beach and the crashing waves in front of us. The sun was slowly setting and had created a beautiful warm glow across the night sky. I really did love this place and was glad I had chosen to bring him. It had been a while since I'd been.

"Yeah, I used to come here a lot," I sighed.

"You *used* to?" he questioned in interest.

"I'm not home much anymore because of my job."

"Are your offices here in St. Petersburg?"

"Yeah. I might need to drop by there tomorrow, actually, and pick up any messages that have been left for me. I'm flying out to Rome next week." Oliver's face dropped. "What is it?"

"I don't like the idea of you being so far away from me. I'll be in New York next week."

"I'm sure we can arrange another get together soon. I could always come to you," I suggested casually, tucking into another part of my lobster.

"You really wouldn't mind traveling to see me?"

"Of course not," I frowned. "Why would I mind?"

"I know I've been intense, asking to stay with you when we've only met once before."

"Did you hear me complaining?"

"No," Oliver smirked, "but I don't want you to think I assumed anything. I'm not usually this demanding."

"You're the billionaire. Shouldn't you be worried more about *me*? What if I'm just after your money?" I teased.

"You're not. I can feel in your body how much you want me. This isn't about my money." I gulped silently as his eyes tried to penetrate my defenses. Keeping my feelings in check had to become a priority. I'd never been this careless before, but Oliver was such an amazing lover, it was difficult to control myself.

"You can read me *that* well?" I muttered, picking up my

bottle of beer.

He winked, licking his lips. "You know I can."

"Okay," I replied, acting flustered. "Let's change the subject and get another beer. Then I'll take you to my favorite bar."

"St. Petersburg's tour *Jade style* it is, then," he winked, downing his drink before getting up to get two more bottles. It seemed my plan to pretend to get drunk just might work tonight.

❈ ❈ ❈

"I think you should slow down, Jade," Oliver chuckled, taking my tenth shot of vodka away from me. He didn't know most of the others had actually been water.

"Dance with me," I purred, running my hands seductively down his chest. Oh, I couldn't wait to get him home. We'd been in the Red Velvet Bar for an hour, and I was so turned on. I could feel the beat of the music through my chest, and all the sweaty bodies on the dance floor were grinding against each other, making me want Oliver even more. I wanted to go crazy on that *fine* body of his.

"*Dance?*" Oliver questioned, raising an eyebrow at me.

"Okay, not just dance," I whispered, crashing my body against his. "I want to rub my sweaty body against yours and then take you home to fuck the crap out of you."

"Jesus Christ, Jade!" Oliver panted, finally letting me pull him into the crowd. I began to grind my ass against his crotch to the beat of the music as soon as his hands soon found their way to my hips. "So, this is the other side of you I've been missing out on, huh?" he groaned into my ear as his hands grazed up and down both sides of my body.

"This is the bolder Jade," I giggled, pretending to stumble a little as I turned around to face him.

"Mm...no, I think this is the *drunk* Jade," Oliver commented, running his hands through my hair. "Maybe I should get you home. You've had more than enough to drink for one night."

"Oh, yes. Home sounds good," I winked, grabbing his ass. He jumped in shock before shaking his head at me.

He gave me a teasing smile as he spoke. "Oh, I'm not going to let you live this down in the morning." I responded by crashing my lips against his, and when he groaned into my mouth, I backed him up against the wall, gripping the tops of his shoulders. I could feel his erection pressed against my stomach, so I slowly ran my hands down his chest, moving lower to cup him. There were so many people in the bar that no one would have noticed what we were doing.

"The only thing you'll be telling me in the morning is how well I can fuck," I snarled, kissing him again and pulling on his bottom lip with my teeth. Oh, it felt good to be able to be myself around him, even if it was only for one night. There was no doubt in my mind that Oliver would be able to take everything I gave him. I felt like a caged beast, and knew that the moment we both stepped inside my apartment, I could be unleashed.

"Who the hell *are* you?" he gasped, "and what have you done with Jade?" I giggled, taking his hand and leading him outside to catch a cab.

"Do you remember fucking me in the back of your limo in London?" I slurred a little. I didn't want to act so drunk that Oliver would feel as if he was taking advantage of me, but I still had to act drunk enough to act so brave.

Being a Seductor was harder than it looked. In a lot of ways, you had to be a really good actress and *become* your character before you really even had the chance to work them out.

"Mm...yeah. That isn't something I could *ever* forget, Jade."

"I wish we could do that right here in this taxi," I giggled, resting my head on his shoulder.

"Maybe we should save car sex for my limo. I'm not sure how the taxi driver would feel if we started getting busy right here."

"True," I sighed, looking up at him. "I *really* like you, Oliver." People always told the truth when they were drunk. The Seductors had taught me a lot about human emotions over the five years I'd worked for them. Alcohol gave you that push to conquer all your fears. It was no wonder I hardly *ever* drank in real life. In my case, it was *all* an act.

"I *really* like you, too, Jade," he smiled. I was definitely going to accomplish my mission. Oliver Kirkham *was* falling for me—I could see it in his eyes.

The moment he closed my front door I pounced on him, groaning into his mouth as I pushed him into my kitchen counter.

"Slow down, Beautiful," he murmured against my lips. I had no intention of listening to him, though.

"What if I don't want to slow down?" I whispered, moving to unbutton his jeans. "What if I've been dying to do something to you, but haven't had the courage until now?" Unhindered by the button, Oliver's jeans fell to the floor.

"Holy shit, Jade," he groaned as I slid my hands into his

boxers.

"You've given me so much pleasure. Why don't you let me lead tonight?" I licked my lips as I felt his member grow even harder in my hands.

"Jade, this isn't you," he smiled sadly. "You'll regret this in the morning. I'm not going to take advantage of you when you're drunk."

"I'm not that drunk," I pouted before smiling seductively as I began to rub his erection up and down with my hand.

"Sweetheart...ugh...stop." Oliver tried to pull my hand out of his boxers, but as I brushed it over the tip of his dick, he threw his head back in pleasure.

"I haven't even started yet," I whispered into his ear, biting down on his earlobe before I dropped to my knees. I pulled his boxers down so I was face-to-face with his impressive length.

"Jade, get up off your knees. I...I can't...let you...oh fuck!" I didn't give Oliver a chance to finish. After licking the precum off the tip of his dick, I took him all the way into my mouth and sucked hard. I didn't waste time teasing him like I really wanted to, though. Instead, I used my teeth to graze his length as I took him deeper into the back of my throat.

Oliver's hands tangled with my hair, his groans and hip thrusts inside my mouth only spurring me on more. I continued to use my teeth and tongue as I slid his hard cock in and out of my mouth. When I felt him begin to pulse, I moved my hands to cup his balls. Within seconds, he came hot and fast down my throat.

I wiped my lips as I looked up at him. "Did you enjoy that?"

"Jesus...fucking...Christ!" He seemed lost for words, and that wasn't even the best blow job I could give.

"I'll take that as a yes," I giggled, standing up while making sure I wobbled a little.

Oliver was gloriously naked in my kitchen, but I needed to get him to my bed—that was when the fun could *really* begin.

"Jade...I...I..." He was still speechless as his breathing began to regulate, so I took his hand with a sly smile and led him to my room. "Is this what you keep fighting?" he asked once we were standing next to my bed.

"Maybe," I giggled, pushing him down on the mattress. "Don't move. You can watch me strip," I hiccupped.

Oliver studied me closely as I slowly removed my dress. I giggled, going *way* over the top with the stripper poses while humming a sexy stripper tune as I removed my underwear.

"God, you're stunning," he moaned when I crawled up his body, letting my long blonde hair tickle his chest.

"Mm...stunning," I grinned, licking his chest before sucking on his left nipple. "How about sexy?"

"Definitely sexy," Oliver exhaled as I dragged my wet sex over his erection.

"I want to make you feel as good as you've made me feel," I purred, straddling him.

"Damn, Jade...you're doing that already, believe me." *Oh no, Oliver. I can do much better than this.*

As I stretched over his chest to grab a condom from my dresser, Oliver's hands glided down my back to cup my ass.

"Are you sure about this, Sweetheart? You've had a lot to drink." He searched my eyes as I sat back up on him.

A wicked smile spread across my face as I ripped the condom open and rolled it over his length. "Does that answer your question?"

Oliver groaned as I sank down onto his erection. "I hope you remember all of this in the morning." *Oh, I will, Oliver. I will.*

"Are you ready to be well and truly fucked?" I purred, rolling my hips against him.

His head fell back into the soft, plush pillows in response.

I have you right where I want you, Oliver Kirkham. Let the fucking commence.

CHAPTER SEVEN

I stretched in bed the next morning only to find it empty. *That wasn't a good sign.* If Oliver had left, I was in *big* trouble. Did I go too far last night? I may have gotten a little carried away, but he thought I was drunk. If he was still here, I would hopefully be able to blame it all on the alcohol.

I quickly pulled on a shirt and some sweats before going in search of him. When my eyes caught sight of him in my kitchen, I sighed in relief. What was he doing…making breakfast?

"Good morning," he grinned, turning to face me. "How's the head?"

"Painful," I lied, moving to get some painkillers from the cabinet above the sink. Oliver had already poured me a glass of cold water from the fridge by the time I turned back around. Sitting on the stool, I winced as I took the pills and water.

"Do you remember much from last night?" he questioned, turning back to the stove. Damn, he could cook and looked *sexy* doing it. That might've had something to do with the fact that Oliver had no shirt on, though.

"I don't remember much after the bar," I lied, yawning.

"You don't remember *anything* that happened back here?" It looked like he was making me an omelet, and I was so hungry my mouth was watering.

"Um…" I blushed, looking down at the marble countertop in front of me. "I remember bits and pieces. I um…remember what I did to you in here."

"You were like another woman last night, Jade. The alcohol…I have no idea what it did to you, but I don't think I've cum that hard—ever—and that was *before* you even got me into your bed." Yeah, I already knew I was *that* good. I was a Seductor, after all.

"Really?" I gasped, looking up at him with wide eyes. "I don't know what came over me. I hardly ever drink."

"You definitely let go last night," Oliver whispered, standing over me. "And it was an amazing sight to behold." I grinned as he leaned down to peck my lips. "How about a little breakfast? You really need to try and eat something to soak up all that alcohol in your system."

"I could try. It smells amazing."

"Omelets are about the only thing I can cook," he chuckled, going back to the stove to dish up. I still found it sexy, and I happened to *love* omelets. "I made some fresh coffee, too. I'll pour you a cup. Why don't you go and sit on the balcony and I'll bring this out to you in a minute."

"You're *my* guest. Shouldn't I be doing all this?"

"I didn't drink my body weight in alcohol last night," Oliver winked. That was a slight exaggeration, but it made me snigger. "No alcohol for you today."

"I agree," I muttered, getting up to wander outside.

Oliver walked out with a tray moments later. "What are our plans for today, seeing as this is our last full day together?"

"I thought I'd take you to that local artist's workshop I was telling you about," I mumbled through a mouthful of omelet.

"Do you mean the one that paints the marina?" I nodded. "Slow down, Jade. You'll get indigestion to go with that hangover if you're not careful," he laughed, watching me eat.

"I'm *really* hungry."

"I can't imagine why. Maybe it's all that mind blowing sex we had last night," Oliver purred, his voice low and husky. It made me choke on my last mouthful. "I'm sorry. I shouldn't have said that," he rebuffed, looking a little embarrassed. "I shouldn't have taken advantage of you last night, either. It was wrong of me to let you get that carried away."

"It sounds like I was the one doing all the *taking* last night. Don't worry about it," I pointed out, looking out toward the sea. "Why don't we finish breakfast and then head out to explore the town? I still have a lot to show you."

"That sounds like a plan," he grinned.

I showered and dressed an hour later. Oliver looked heavenly in his faded ripped jeans and pale blue shirt as he stood waiting for me to finish.

"You still look beautiful—even with a hangover," he teased, pecking my lips.

"I'm feeling much better after taking a shower."

"Mm...you have no idea how hard it was for me not to join you," he winked, running his hands down my back, "but I thought we might need a few hours off from *that*."

"Just a few hours?"

"I leave in the morning, Jade, and I plan on having you at least another two times before I go. I'm not sure when I'll see you again, after all." Oliver really was sex crazed.

"Well, we better get the sightseeing over with then, huh?"

"I think it might be wise." I wasn't sure if he was being serious right now or not.

We took the elevator down to the private garage to get my car.

"A Mercedes Benz E Class Convertible—I should have guessed," Oliver mused as I walked to the driver's side. "Where do you think you're going?"

"Um…I'm driving us around. Why do you think I brought you down here?"

"You're not driving anywhere. You're still under the influence." *Like hell I was. Nobody drove my* baby *but me!*

"I'll be fine," I pouted, going to open the door.

"Jade," Oliver threatened. *Damn it!* I huffed, throwing him the keys. "Good girl," he chuckled, kissing me when we passed each other as we were changing sides.

When we were both seated I asked, "Do you even know how to drive? I can't imagine you driving yourself that much."

"I can drive, Jade. You're safe," he laughed, putting his sunglasses on. Sexy didn't even *begin to cover* how good he looked.

He turned the engine over, reminding me how loud my music had been the last time I'd driven. *When We Were Young* by The Killers was blasting out of the speakers.

"Sorry," I giggled, quickly turning it down.

"The Killers, huh?" Oliver mused, resting his arm on my seat while he looked behind us to back out.

"They're legends." That was the truth; I loved The Killers. Well, I loved most rock music, to be honest.

"I have to agree. You have great taste in music. I saw all your classic rock CDs back at your apartment, too." He reached his hand out, turning the volume back up. My jaw went slack as I sat there listening to him sing along to the song. *What a liar!* He wasn't tone deaf—his voice was actually pretty *good*.

Why did I see a hidden meaning when Oliver started to sing the part about 'sitting waiting for some beautiful boy to save you from your old ways'? Deep down, did I want to be saved? It wouldn't matter if I did. Even if I *was* falling for Oliver and wanted him to save me, there wasn't anything I could do about it. If he knew the real me, he wouldn't want me anyway. "Sing with me, Jade. I'm not doing this solo," Oliver yelled over the music, snapping me from my thoughts. I laughed but quickly joined in.

I felt so carefree, cruising down the highway with the wind in my hair, singing along to a song that suddenly had so much more meaning than it used to.

"Your car drives really well," Oliver stated once we were parked. "And I love the color. It matches your eyes."

"Thanks." We were heading to my 'office' first because Sonia had instructions for me on a case I needed to do with Molly in Rome next week.

"Did you want to come up?" I asked as I stood outside the building.

"Only if you want me to." I could tell by the look on his face that he was intrigued to see where I worked. Plus, it would only strengthen my cover.

"Honestly, Oliver, if you want to come up, that's fine. My boss is out of the country. It's only Molly in the office today."

"Who's Molly?" he asked, following me inside.

"The receptionist and my boss' personal assistant," I called over my shoulder.

The office was on the third floor, so we opted to use the elevator. I was secretly glad because, if I was being honest, I was a little sore from our activities.

Molly was behind her desk when we arrived, and I had to fight back a giggle. She'd dyed her hair a deep red and was wearing thick black glasses. *Oh, Molly was the master of disguise.* She was so funny.

"Good morning, Miss Gibbs. How are you enjoying your time off?" She greeted me with a friendly smile before her eyes moved to Oliver. They almost bulged out of her head as she took him in.

"I'm having a wonderful break, thank you," I smirked, winking at her when she looked back at me. "This is Oliver, a friend of mine who is staying with me for a few days. Oliver, this is Molly."

"Lovely to meet you, Oliver," Molly said a little breathlessly.

"And you, Molly," Oliver replied, darting his eyes to me.

"I'll get Molly to make you some coffee. You can take a seat here, if you'd like. I'm just going to check my emails in my office —I'll be right back." I smiled at Oliver before leaving Molly to ask him how he took his coffee.

"Holy shit!" Molly walked into my fake office minutes later. "*That's* your target? Jesus, Jade! Just looking at him would give me an orgasm. You lucky bitch! You wait until I tell Georgie when she gets back this week."

"Well hello, Molly. It's nice to see you, too," I sniggered. Georgie was on her way home—thank God!

"Sorry," she laughed, taking her glasses off. "How's it all going?"

"Good. Did Sonia give you the flight details for Rome?"

"Yep." Molly placed a file on the desk. "Did you get the mission email, too? It looks like an easy steal, but the target likes to pick his prostitutes in pairs." *Great! I hated playing a prostitute.*

"What are we going after?"

"It's a slander campaign. We need pictures." *Oh, my favorite kind of mission.* NOT! "I know you hate missions like this, Jade, but we do them so well together."

"Who is the target—another politician?" I yawned.

"Yeah," Molly muttered. "We leave Sunday morning. Shall I meet you at headquarters or the airport?"

"Headquarters. I need to pick up some clothes and report back to Sonia on the status of this mission. It means I can see Georgie, too, before we go."

"Is this guy rich?"

"You know you shouldn't be prying, Molly," I tutted.

"Everyone is talking about how huge this mission is back at headquarters, so I can't help it. It must be so exciting. I can't wait to get targets like him." She had a ways to go before Sonia trusted her with the top targets. That was something that was earned through hard work and proven loyalty.

I picked up the paper with flight details for Rome and placed it in my bag. It was safe—it only had my contact name and my boarding pass. Molly would keep all the mission related information back at headquarters until we needed it.

"You never did say if this Oliver guy is any good in bed." There was a reason for that. "He looks like the kind of guy that knows what he's doing."

"Just try and keep your jaw closed when you say goodbye to him. I think I saw you drool a little when we arrived," I teased, nudging her.

"Bitch," she muttered under her breath as we walked back into the reception area.

Oliver was just sitting there waiting for me. "Did you get everything sorted?" he grinned, standing up.

"Yeah," I beamed, looking at Molly who was still gawking at him. For a Seductor, she had a lot to learn. "We can go now."

"Nice meeting you, Molly," Oliver called back as we turned to leave, and I swear I heard her mutter something like, '*Please come back soon.*'

"What?" Oliver asked as I shook my head while getting into my car.

"What the hell did you do to the receptionist?" I giggled. "I've never seen Molly that excited before."

"I have no idea what you mean," he snorted, pulling back onto the highway as we made our way to the marina.

* * *

"Jerry has an amazing use of tone," I whispered into Oliver's ear while we stood studying the paintings. We were visiting the local artist studio I'd told him about earlier. "His pieces are quite bold, too, so they might not be what you're looking for."

"No, they're amazing—very moving," he muttered, still lost in the painting. "I can't decide whether to take that canvas or the large one you showed me in the back." Wow, he wasn't joking about liking the pieces. "You really do have an eye for art, Jade. Taking away the fact that I can't keep my hands off you, I would still really like you to take a look at my properties and help me redesign my office in New York." Oliver's office was in New York, and I couldn't help but wonder if that was where he kept his hard drive.

"Redesign your entire office?"

"You've obviously studied interior design and spent a lot of time on it to be where you are. Besides, I love the idea of sitting in an office you've designed. It might make it easier for me when we're apart," he teased, wrapping his arms around my waist.

"That's a huge job, Oliver," I pointed out.

"Mm…would it mean a lot of meetings?"

"Yes," I laughed, hitting his chest. "But honestly, there are better Interior Designers than me. I can help you with your art pieces, though—that isn't an issue."

"No," Oliver replied sternly. "I want you and no one else." I wasn't sure Oliver was talking about my interior design skills anymore, judging by the intensity of his gaze.

"I'll have to check my schedule and make some space to visit you in New York, then," I sighed, looking back at the painting. "If you like both paintings, why don't you buy them both? I could use them as the color scheme for your new office." He didn't need much convincing, and within the hour, he'd paid forty thousand dollars for the two canvases.

"You look like you want to ask me something," he commented as we sat down to have a late lunch in a small diner later that afternoon.

"You don't act like you're a billionaire. Why is that?"

Oliver's eyes widened for an instant before he spoke. "I may have been born into this money, Jade, but I won't let that determine who I really am. Yes, I'm a very wealthy businessman, and that comes with certain obligations, but I want to *live*, as well. My job isn't easy, and I need a separate life from it. "

"What type of machines does your company make? It would have to be something big if it involves you having to meet with world leaders. Are you saving the environment or something?" I asked innocently. All of this was my plan to get him to trust me—poor innocent Jade, who knew nothing about the top secret weapons his company was making.

Oliver let out a deep laugh. "Oh, Jade, I wish I was, believe me. My company makes weapons, mainly."

"Weapons?" I gasped. My mouth went slack and I acted shocked. "You mean like guns and rifles?"

"No, we make larger weapons than that, Beautiful," he said as he swallowed hard. "I should have told you in London, but I didn't want to overload you with information and scare you away."

"What kind of weapons do you make, Oliver?" My voice was just a whisper.

"Weapons that are only used for purposes of defense. Every country needs to be able to protect itself and its residents against outside threats. It's their defensive strategies that stop wars from breaking out most of the time, and my company plays a small part in that." It was obvious that he was trying to defend himself before he'd even admitted that his company made nuclear weapons.

"Oliver, stop stalling—just tell me."

"My company makes the machines that can load nuclear weapons, Jade."

"Oh." I sat there staring at him, eyes wide, jaw slack.

"Say something, please? I've been trying to find a way to explain this since I arrived the other day. It's my job, Jade, but it doesn't define who I am. I have to protect my company, though. I don't trust anyone else to do it. Some of the information I have would be disastrous in the wrong hands."

"Give me a second. It's just a lot to take in. When you said *machines*, I never thought..."

"I know. I should have explained it better and I'm sorry." Oliver reached across the table to grab my hand. "I don't want this to come between us."

"I have to admit, I hardly know anything about nuclear weapons—just what I learned in school."

"I'd be happy to explain if that's what you want."

"No. I think I'd rather be in the dark about most of it. Like you said—your job doesn't define you," I interrupted, taking a sip of my drink. "At least I understand all the meetings with the world leaders now. What do you do, play them against each other to get the highest price?"

Oliver choked on his drink. "No, Jade. Out of the five primary countries that deal in nuclear weapons, there are only three I would *ever* do business with. My company makes weapons strictly for defensive purposes. I worry that if we sold it to the wrong country, they would use my weapons as a scare tactic, instead."

"It all sounds incredibly stressful." I exhaled deeply, playing it up.

"Why else do you think I've spent all these years looking for you?" he muttered, reaching over the table for my hand again. "With you, I can let go for a little while. No one has ever relaxed me as much as you have, Beautiful." He did seem more carefree around me, and I had to admit that he wasn't the typical CEO of a multi-billion dollar company. I had met my fair share of those in the last five years as a Seductor, and none of them had made me feel the things he had.

"Oliver, it's been no time at all since we met. You can't pin all your hopes on one person." Why was I warning him about me? I should have been happy with what he was saying—I was doing my job and I was succeeding.

"I know, but no one has ever made me feel the way you do, Jade. I'm even dreading having to leave in the morning."

I should have been happy with Oliver's statement but I wasn't. Instead, I felt a huge ache in my chest at his confession.

CHAPTER EIGHT

Oliver and I went back to my penthouse after lunch.

Sometimes the best way to answer untold questions was to simply feel skin against skin. That was something I had learned before I became a Seductor.

Being wrapped up in Oliver's arms after hours of lovemaking seemed like the best answer to me right now. It was the only thing that *did* make sense.

"You'll try and come to New York as soon as you can, right?" he murmured, running his hands up and down my bare back.

"I'll see if I can move a few clients around to fit you in." I stretched, running my nails across his chest.

"I'm sorry to be so demanding."

"Oliver, stop. I want to see you again soon, too," I exhaled, moving to straddle him.

"Mm…this position is bringing back some great memories." He gently trailed his hands up my body and palmed my breasts, leaving goose bumps in his wake. "If you want to take the lead again, Jade, I'm fine with that."

"I think I'll take a rain check, but thanks."

"Not drunk enough, huh?" Oh, he thought he was *so*

funny.

"No," I giggled as he stroked my cheek lovingly. "I'm just as spellbound in all of this as you are, you know. I don't want you to leave tomorrow, and I'm dreading going to Rome next week. All I really want to do is stay right here with you."

"The world would still turn if we stayed here, I'm sure of it. We could if you really wanted to," he smoldered, running his fingertips down into my sex. I couldn't stop myself from rocking against his hand. "That's it, Beautiful, feel it." I threw my head back, groaning as Oliver sat up to capture one of my nipples with his mouth. He twirled his tongue around the hardened peak, pulling it gently with his teeth before using his fingers to penetrate me deeply.

"Ugh...so good..." I yearned, rocking faster against his hand.

"You wait until my dick is back inside you. Then you'll feel *good*," he whispered, pulling a condom out and ripping it open with his teeth. With a teasing grin, he motioned to his length and the condom. "Would you do the honors?"

"With pleasure," I giggled.

"After this, I promise we'll get dinner," he winked, pushing me down onto his length.

"Don't worry," I moaned, becoming lost in the sensation. "We can have takeout in bed if we have to." Oliver seemed to like that idea, because he set a fast, wild pace.

* * *

We were disturbed an hour later by my intercom being pressed over and over again. *Who the hell could that be?* I frowned down at Oliver before quickly pulling on some clothes.

"Are you expecting anyone?" he asked, sitting up in bed.

"No," I muttered, wandering over to the intercom. "Hello?"

"I need to speak with Mario right away. It's urgent. I found this address in some paperwork he left at my place," a frantic female voice said. It had to be Mario's target from the mission he'd just completed. Great, that was all I needed right now.

"I'm sorry, but Mario doesn't live here anymore. He hasn't for the last eight months," I replied, watching Oliver come over to me with a confused look on his face.

"I'm not leaving until I see for myself. I need to speak to him. That bastard might have cost me my job!"

"Annette, is that you?" I seethed, deciding to play the scorned girlfriend. I could even use Mario as an excuse to Oliver as to why I was always so guarded.

"Who is this?" the voice replied, obviously confused.

"It's Jade. You know, the woman whose boyfriend you stole! He isn't here, but if he cost you your job, then I would say karma came back to bite you in the ass! The two of you deserve everything you get!"

"How do I know you're not hiding him in there? Jade, this is fucking serious. I think he's done something really bad," Annette screeched over the intercom.

I was about to reply when Oliver pulled me out of the way. "I suggest you leave right now before we call the cops. Jade has already informed you that he isn't here," Oliver replied sternly, rubbing my back softly in an attempt to soothe me.

"Who the hell is this?"

"That is none of your business, but I suggest you leave right now and look for this Mario elsewhere. He. Is. Not. Here."

I could hear Annette mumble something unintelligible over the intercom before finally speaking.

"Okay, but Jade, if you do hear from him, please..."

"Jade doesn't owe you any favors, and I think you are out of line to even ask," Oliver interrupted. "Goodbye." With that, he ended the conversation.

"Would you care to explain what the hell just happened?" he questioned, turning and raising an eyebrow at me.

"Mario is an ex...really. It's nothing," I smiled nervously, going to my fridge to get some fresh orange juice. "Do you want some juice?"

"It doesn't seem like *nothing* to me. How long were the two of you together?" God, the thought of Mario and me *actually* together made me throw up in my mouth a little.

"Two years," I exhaled, pouring us both a drink. "He started working at the same company as Annette about a year ago, and well, they had an affair behind my back." Oliver's eyes saddened as he watched me. "It's okay, though. I'm over it. I took control of the rent for this place and kicked him out over eight months ago."

"Did you love him?" he asked, sitting on one of my kitchen stools.

"I thought I did at the time." I smiled sadly, shaking my head while trying to be more upbeat. Heartbreak was an easy emotion for me to portray.

"I guess that explains a few things about you," Oliver mused, watching me closely. "Did Mario ever make you feel the things I can?" A seductive smile spread across his face, and I grinned back as I walked up to him and slid between his legs.

"No one has *ever* made me feel the things you can," I

purred, running my hands through his hair.

"It's our last night together for a while, Jade. How about we make the most of it?" I closed my eyes at the feel of Oliver's hands. He ran them down my legs before grabbing my hips, pulling me closer to him as he crashed his lips against mine. With one kiss, I surrendered.

* * *

Our three days together went by way too fast. Oliver was standing by the front door saying goodbye to me, and a small part of me really didn't want him to go.

"I'll call you when I land, and please let me know that you've arrived safely when you get to Rome next week," he murmured, running his hands through my hair. "Thank you for an amazing few days."

"I should be thanking you," I whispered, grabbing the collar of his white shirt and pulling him to me.

Oliver smiled, leaning down to give me a soft yet passionate kiss. "I'm counting the days until I see you again, Beautiful." My arms found their way around his neck as our tongues began a slow and sensual dance.

"I'm missing you already," I breathed against his lips as the kiss broke. With a longing look and one last kiss, he left.

* * *

"You've done well, Jade," Sonia commented, flipping through my notes on my findings so far. "I am assuming you'll try and gain access to his office in New York first?"

"It seems the most logical place for the hard drive to be stored."

"What about his family home in Macon, Georgia?"

"That would be my next choice, but I think New York will be the easiest to infiltrate. Mr. Kirkham wants me to redesign his office there."

"Oh, Jade. No wonder you're number one around here. You're so ruthless and you do it effortlessly." I used to think that, but doubt had slowly started to creep into my mind.

"Is that all you need from me, Sonia?" I asked, stretching. I was eager to find Molly; we had a fight to catch in less than three hours.

"I think you've covered everything so far. Thank you." Sonia smiled from behind her desk. "Keep up the good work." I nodded before getting up to leave.

* * *

Molly was lying across her bed when I walked into our shared room. "Are you even packed yet?" I complained.

"Jeez, you scared the shit out of me," she gasped, holding her chest. "Of course I've already packed. I was just waiting for you."

"Do you have the information file?" I asked, collecting a few items from my closet that I'd forgotten to take to the penthouse.

"Yep. It's already packed. Are you ready?"

"Yeah, I just need to pack a few dresses and my thigh highs."

"I'm excited to be getting out for a few days. Mario has

been unbearable this week. Did you hear that his last target has been trying to track him down? He's on lockdown for a *month*." Lockdown wasn't easy—you couldn't leave headquarters for any reason—but sometimes with the larger missions, there was no other choice. I suspected the same would happen to me once I'd completed my mission with Oliver. I didn't feel sorry for Mario, though; I didn't like the guy enough for that.

"I know. She came by the penthouse last week."

"While your target was there?" Molly choked. "What did you do?"

"I used it to my advantage," I winked, packing the last few things away.

"Here are my girls!" I heard Georgie before I saw her, but I screeched like a schoolgirl and rushed over to hug her when she came into view. It had been almost two months since she'd been back at headquarters. Georgie was a redhead with the most beautiful green eyes I'd ever seen, and her skin was like pure snow. She was absolutely stunning, and my best friend in The Seductors. I wasn't sure how I would get by in this job without her. We could talk about anything and everything, and often did. Georgie was the only person I trusted with my life.

"Georgie, I am so glad you're back," I beamed.

"I heard you two are heading out on a mission together?"

"Yeah. We need to leave soon, but when we get back, you and I can catch up."

"Sounds good to me," Georgie winked. "It's good to see you, Jelly Bean."

"You've been spending too much time with Drew," I chuckled.

"You know I love that name for you." She smiled and then

reached up to stroke my hair. "Your hair has grown a lot. I wish mine was this silky."

"You have amazing hair," I commented, trying to play off her compliment. Georgie knew she was stunning, and if she wanted to talk about soft silky hair...well, she had it, not me.

"As much as I love listening to you two talk about your hair all day, Jade and I have a flight to catch," Molly interrupted sarcastically.

"Okay, let's go," I sighed, grabbing my suitcase while rolling my eyes at Georgie as she smirked back.

"Knock 'em dead, ladies," Georgie replied, slapping both mine and Molly's ass as we walked past her.

"Yay!" Molly giggled as we loaded our bags into the car. "A mini-vacation with Jade." I had to chuckle. This was anything *but* a vacation. I was just glad to have some time away from Oliver. When I did see him again, my mind would hopefully be back on the mission instead of thinking about all the wonderful things he could do to me with his hands and tongue.

❊ ❊ ❊

"You look hot in that dress," Molly muttered as we were shown into the hotel suite where our target was waiting for us. Michael Roswell was a well-known English Politician who was in Rome as part of an environmental conference this week.

Slander campaigns were big business to *The Seductors*. In recent years, most scandals of a sexual nature had been started by one of us.

"Thanks," I laughed, running my hands down the thin red fabric. The dress didn't leave much to the imagination, but

Molly and I were supposed to be prostitutes. She looked stunning herself in a tight black leather dress. We were both playing our parts well tonight.

"Are you leading this one, or am I?"

"I don't mind either way," I shrugged. "I've already had a lot of action lately, so if you want to lead, you can."

"You lucky bitch. What I wouldn't give to be able to jump up and down on Oliver's dick. I bet it's huge, isn't it?" Molly never was known for her tact.

"You'll never know," I giggled as we finally arrived at the suite.

After our fake IDs were checked, we were shown in by security. Mr. Roswell was already sitting on the couch waiting for us. Politicians—they were always so eager.

"Good evening, ladies," he welcomed us. "My, I've picked well tonight."

"Do you want us here or in the bedroom?" Molly asked, dropping her bag on the table. Following suit, I did the same. I would grab my small camera later when Mr. Roswell was somewhat distracted.

"The bedroom I think," he grinned, getting up while already starting to unbutton his shirt. He was practically undressed by the time we reached the bedroom. "Okay, you can suck me off." He motioned to Molly, for which I was extremely grateful. "And you can strip down and I'll pleasure you," he commented toward me. His eyes roamed my body darkly and I had to fight back the urge to throw up. Maybe Molly *had* gotten the better deal after all. We were both quick to obey his orders— after all, we were supposed to be prostitutes.

Molly rid Mr. Roswell of his boxers, pushed him down onto

bed, and began to suck him off immediately. His eyes rolled back into his head as she engulfed his length in her mouth while I stripped out of my dress. Mr. Roswell's eyes flashed to mine the moment I began to remove my underwear. "That's it, Sexy, bring your hot pussy over to me," he yearned, fighting against the pleasure Molly was already giving him. I stalked over to him once I was naked and sat on his chest with my legs either side of him. His hands ran over my breasts, grabbing them roughly.

These were the times I felt dead inside. It numbed the pain of having strangers touch me so intimately. "Let's see how wet you are, Sexy." He wasn't a good looking guy by any means, but I couldn't even close my eyes to try and make it more enjoyable because all I saw when I did was Oliver's face. Mr. Roswell dipped his fingers into my sex, running them up and down my clit. It was nowhere near fast enough, but playing my cover, I groaned and threw my head back to make him think I was enjoying it.

Looking behind, I saw Molly making slow, long licks up and down his length before sucking the tip into her mouth and swirling her tongue around him.

"Fuck, you girls are good," Mr. Roswell moaned, pulling me down toward him so he could invade my mouth with his tongue. He reeked of cigarettes and his kiss was wet and sloppy. I was tempted to wipe my mouth once he pulled away, but I stopped myself. Instead, I continued pretending that I was coming undone under his hands as he began to thrust two fingers inside me. Once I knew he was about to explode in Molly's mouth, I clenched my pelvic muscles around his fingers and groaned loudly, faking my release. Mr. Roswell climaxed right after with a string of grunts.

Molly wiped her mouth, winking at me while our target

came back down to earth.

"Which one of us do you want to fuck first?" I purred, running my hands down his chest. "I've just cum thanks to your amazing fingers, so maybe my friend should get her release next?" He seemed conflicted as his hands ran up and down my body before playing with my nipples. *Oh, please choose Molly first. I'd rather take the damn pictures.*

Together, Molly and I were most guys' fantasy—the kinky brunette and the sexy blonde. Deciding which of us to start with was a hard choice to make for most.

"I'll fuck your friend first from behind, but when I get to you, I want you on top riding the shit of me. For now, you can sit there and play with yourself while you watch us." He gestured toward the chair next to the bed, something so predictable. Most Politicians were *dirty perverts!*

"Can I use your bathroom first?" I asked, watching him turn Molly so she was on all fours. He'd pulled her dress up around her hips and was slowly pulling her panties down.

"Make it quick," he ordered, looking at Molly's ass as he stroked it. I could hear the sound of foil and knew that by the time I came back in, he'd be fucking her.

I grabbed the small camera on the way back from the bathroom. Mr. Roswell was slamming hard into Molly from behind. Well, hard for him—I'd seen more force from a dog that was practically knocking at death's door.

I snapped a few photos of them before I sat down in the chair. He was so engrossed in Molly as she thrust back against him that he didn't even notice I'd come back. It was sad, really; the poor girl was trying to find her own release but was struggling. After setting a timer, I put the camera down at an angle on the dresser beside me. Every few minutes, it would automatically take a picture. The gadgets we used were so unrecognizable and ordinary that our targets hardly ever questioned them. The camera itself looked like a small silver pen.

"You're not touching yourself. I want your pussy nice and wet for me when you fuck me," Mr. Roswell ordered when he noticed I was back. He was trying to slam hard into Molly again. When my eyes met with hers, she gave me a look that said, 'I'm so bored.'

I began to run my hands over my clit as I spread my legs, giving him full view of my sex. I'd done it for so many strangers in the past that it never bothered me anymore.

Closing my eyes, I was able to forget that anyone was watching me and became lost in my own touch. I hadn't climaxed since...well, since *Oliver*. As he crept into my mind, I was submerged in images of all the things he'd done to me. How his skin felt against mine, his strong, hard body hovering over me as we made love. I'd never cum so fast in my life.

When I opened my eyes, Molly gave me a questioning look. *Yes, Molly, I really just came. Deal with it!*

She began to fake her own orgasm, fisting her hands into the sheets in front of her. Mr. Roswell hadn't climaxed yet, and something told me that he wanted *me* to do that for him. *Great! Lucky me.*

"I'll be sure to ask for you two when I visit Rome again," he panted as Molly moved onto her back. She giggled when he leaned down to capture one of her nipples in his mouth, sucking hard. "Your friend's pussy looks very tasty," he muttered to Molly as he gazed at me. I was still making lazy small circles with my hands because he hadn't actually told me to stop playing with myself yet. "I think I should taste it before I let her fuck me. What do you think?"

"We're yours for an hour. You can do whatever you want," Molly replied, stretching out on the bed.

"Okay, I want you to play with her tits while I eat her pussy. Let's make her scream with pleasure." Sorry, Mr. Roswell. That is *never* going to happen. It's a good thing that I'm a fantastic faker. "Come over here, Sexy, and lie down with us." I gave him an alluring smile and got up. As soon as my head hit the mattress, my legs were parted and he was between them, trying to lap up my juices. I had to fight back the urge to giggle. This man had *no* idea how to please a woman. I actually felt sorry for his wife. Molly watched my expression and smirked before leaning in, pulling at my left nipple with her teeth. I arched my back, pretending it was all too much to take. "Hold still, Sexy," he muttered from between my legs. "I want you nice and wet." The two of them carried out their 'torture' for ten minutes, and I was less than impressed with Mr. Roswell's oral skills.

"Are you ready for me to ride you now, Sir?" I asked innocently, batting my eyelashes at him when he'd finished. I had to laugh, thinking of all the photos we'd gotten of him without him even knowing.

"Yes, Sexy, I am," he replied, turning to lie on his back. "Your friend can sit and watch this time while she plays with herself." *Lucky Molly*.

I grinned, putting a condom on his length before making him climax in less than three minutes. I'd already had more than enough of the asshole.

* * *

Molly and I were quick to get changed as soon as his hour was up. While Mr. Roswell used the restroom, I placed the small camera back in my bag.

He tipped us well with three hundred dollars, and without another word, we left. The photos would quickly be leaked to the press, and poor Mr. Roswell would probably have charges filed against him by this time next week. Part of me wondered what his wife and children were going to think about the pictures, not that I really cared. Molly's and my face would be altered or hidden before anything was released. Plus, there might even be a nice bonus in it for each of us if the story went global.

"What was all that in the chair earlier?" Molly questioned on our way back to our hotel. "You actually came. What the fuck were you thinking about?"

"Don't be silly." I brushed off her comment and tried to act natural.

"Or maybe I should ask *who*?"

"I'm a good faker. You know that."

"Has this Oliver guy actually made you cum by his own hands?" she persisted. "You've had this goofy look on your face since you met him." She was such a liar. *Goofy expression my ass!*

"You know we can't talk about my target, Molly," I stressed.

"We're not talking about the mission. I want to know if he's made you cum. You've never cum at the hands of a target before, and if that's changed—this is *huge*."

"Yes, okay? Oliver has made me cum more times than I can

count!" I whined, trying to put an end to the interrogation.

"Holy shit!" Molly gasped, covering her mouth. "Jade, this is fucking epic! You *have* to tell Georgie when we get home!"

"No, it's really not!"

"Oh, you need to be careful. You can't allow yourself to get attached." *Molly* was giving *me* advice now? What the hell?

"I know that, and I'm not attached. Oliver is just extremely good at sex—that's all."

"I knew it!" she replied smugly.

"I have it covered, Molly, trust me. I know what I'm doing."

"I'm glad he's your target." I tilted my head, silently urging her to continue. "If he'd been mine, I would have already fallen for him, and we all know how dangerous *that* is." I smiled at her nervously. "You haven't fallen for him, have you, Jade?"

"Of course not," I laughed, pushing her lightly. "Now, let's go and get shit-faced with our tip from Mr. Roswell. I don't know about you, but he was one of the worst lays I've *ever* had."

Molly giggled in response, wrapping her arm around me. "He was pretty hopeless. Come on, let's line the drinks up at the bar. You're right—we deserve it."

At least the alcohol would silence my mind for a little while.

Was I falling for Oliver? All I knew was that I missed him... a lot.

CHAPTER NINE

"How was Rome?" Oliver asked over the phone. I was currently sitting on my balcony in St. Petersburg, happy, for once, to be home.

"It was okay," I sighed, playing with the toast I'd made myself for breakfast.

"Have you managed to shuffle things around on your client calendar to fit me in yet?"

"I might have," I giggled, rolling my eyes even though he couldn't see me.

"Don't keep me in suspense, Jade," Oliver pleaded.

"I can fit you in the week after next."

"Really? For how long?" He was excited.

"A week, if you need me that long."

"The entire week! Are you being serious? "

"Do you really think I would tease you about this?" I pointed out.

"You've just made my day, Beautiful. I'm going to spoil you rotten when you get here, and I don't just mean with gifts." In between my legs began to tingle because I knew exactly what Oliver meant.

"I can't wait."

"Listen, I have to go. I have a meeting at nine. I'll try and call you tomorrow, though, since I'll be tied up all day today."

"It's fine. You don't have to call me every day, you know," I laughed.

"I know, but I want to. I'm used to hearing your voice every day now."

"So, it's just my voice you want?" I teased.

"You know that isn't true. I miss a lot more than just your voice," Oliver purred. "Have you had any more trouble from that crazy Annette woman?"

"No, but I can handle it. Stop worrying so much."

"I'm sorry, I can't help it."

"You don't need to worry about me. I'm a big girl and can look after myself." In more ways than he would ever know.

"Okay, but if you did need me to help, I…"

"Go to your meeting and call tomorrow if you can," I ordered. Otherwise, I knew we'd be on the phone for another half hour and Oliver would be *really* late for his meeting.

"Okay," he chuckled. "I get it. You can handle the crazy woman. Bye, Beautiful."

"Yes I can. I'll speak to you later." I sighed, shaking my head at this crazy situation. I was glad I had a few small missions to keep me busy over the next few weeks.

* * *

"How am I doing?" Zara asked, walking into the side room that I was currently hiding in.

"Really good," I smiled. Sonia had been giving me small side jobs all week, and I was thankful for once. It didn't stop

Oliver from entering my mind, though. My body was yearning to be touched by him again.

"Does it feel like you're watching a porno?"

"Not really, Zara," I snorted. This girl was really growing on me. She was so funny. "I was having some sound issues, but everything is working now."

"Oh, good."

"Remember, you need a confession out of him. Don't make it all about the sex. Open up to him a little and I'm sure he'll start to talk," I muttered, checking the hallway on my monitoring screen, making sure her target wasn't on his way back up to the hotel room.

"How do I open up to him?"

"Make something up, or tell him about your past if you really want to."

"What would you do?"

"It depends on the target and the situation. No mission is ever the same. Just go with your instincts. They've gotten you this far."

"Okay," she breathed, checking her makeup and then heading back before her target returned.

Zara had been assigned to a local drug dealer. The Seductors were hired to gain a confession from him that confirmed he had been stealing from the shipments and selling the product off to smaller dealers.

Our client base was very varied. It was one of the things I liked about the Seductors. You never knew what mission you'd be assigned to next. It kept things interesting for us.

Today, I was Zara's surveillance. Together, we'd set up cameras in the room before her target had arrived. She had been on this case for two weeks, and I was impressed at how she was handling it. I could see great things for Zara if she kept on the way she was.

She reminded me of a younger version of myself. I'd been fearless when I first started, too. With my past, I had no fear left in me, though. The moment I became a Seductor, I left everything else behind.

"Fuck, Baby, yes! Right there," Zara's target groaned as she began to ride him through his orgasm.

"Shit," Zara panted, collapsing on his chest. "That was amazing."

"I told you it would be," he gloated, running his hands through her sweaty blonde hair.

She did as I had advised and began talking about wanting to get out of town, but not knowing where to go. Her target began showing off his wealth, telling her he could help with the extra money he had been earning. Zara had a confession from him within an hour.

"How did I do?" she asked while I was driving her back to headquarters.

"You were brilliant. I couldn't have done it better myself."

"It must be hard being number one. Do you ever worry someone will knock you off your perch?"

"Someone will one day. I won't always be a Seductor, though, so it doesn't worry me. I never joined to be the best. I just wanted to make some real money. You need to think about what you want from this job. You can set yourself up for life if you plan carefully. It's all about being able to show Sonia you can handle the high earning targets."

"You've got a high earner now, right?"

"Yes."

"Is it exciting?" It was more than exciting. In fact, I couldn't wait to see Oliver again. Was I already in over my head? I forced that thought back, unwilling to think too hard about it. Of course I wasn't in over my head. It was *just* sex!

"Yes, but you have to really focus. The top missions are high paying for a reason. You have to put everything you have into them."

"I hope I'm as good as you in five years' time, Jade," she sighed.

"Judging by how well you're doing now, I have no doubt that you will be, Zara," I grinned, pulling into the parking garage at headquarters.

I wasn't lying, either. I had the feeling Zara was the next me in the making.

* * *

"There's something different about you." Georgie frowned as she sat on my kitchen stool scrutinizing me.

"You shouldn't listen to Molly," I complained. "You know she talks crap half the time." Georgie had dropped by the penthouse to see me before she flew out to her next mission. I was flying out to New York tomorrow, so we weren't sure when we'd see each other next.

"She's just worried about you, Jade. This mission is clearly affecting you, and that's not normal. You're always so focused."

"I'm fine," I sighed. I hated that Georgie could see right through me.

"Sure you are," she mused. "He stayed here, right?"

"Yes. What does that have to do with anything?"

"You don't think it's a little too personal? He was around your things. It makes you vulnerable. The real you, I mean."

"G, you know as well as I do that we all play a part. That's what Seductors are good at. How can I be vulnerable when it isn't the real me? I'm shy, insecure Jade with him."

"So he hasn't seen the real you?"

"Trust me, he has no idea what I'm really like," I chuckled.

"What is it with rich guys and shy women?" She had a point there. "You'd think they'd want a vixen...someone who could take away all the pressures of their jobs when they got home."

"I don't know, but he seems to like my act." I smirked, thinking back to the last time we'd been together.

"*Are* you falling for him?" Where the hell did that come from?

"What?" I choked, widening my eyes at her. "Of course not. This is my job! I'd never put myself in that kind of danger."

"You need to be careful. You know Miss S doesn't take this kind of shit lightly. She'll come down on your ass hard if she finds out."

"There is nothing going on. I'm fine!" I snapped.

"Uh huh. Judging by that reaction, I'm gonna have to call bullshit." Damn Georgie.

"Look, did you come to spend the afternoon with me or not? I don't want to waste the entire day talking about my target."

"Okay. Let's go out to lunch, then," Georgie grinned. "If you say everything is fine, then it must be fine." I knew she was calling my bluff. The truth, though, was that I couldn't even admit to myself how much things had changed, let alone tell Georgie.

"Please don't worry. I'm fine, I promise."

"Who else is going to worry about you, Jelly Bean?"

"I know, I know." I sighed deeply, knowing that I was alone in the world. I had no one, and Georgie knew that better than anyone. "I'm being careful, I swear. It's just like any other mission."

"Keep telling yourself that," she snorted. "Maybe you'll even start to believe it."

"Can we just go to lunch, please?" I stressed. "We both fly out tomorrow, and I need to relax."

"What's the sex like with him?"

"Oh. My. God! Georgie! Shut the fuck up," I fumed.

"It was just a question. Jeez, you're touchy today."

"Stop bugging me, then," I glared. "Can we go already?"

"After you, Miss Moody," she winked.

With a muttered *bitch* under my breath and a smirk on my face, I walked past her. I was thankful she didn't ask any more questions during lunch.

All I had to worry about when I got back was packing for New York; everything else could wait. I knew, though, that when I returned and saw Georgie again, she would probably have more questions for me.

* * *

I sat impatiently as I waited for the plane to touch down in New York. It hadn't been a long flight, but after three grueling weeks of not seeing Oliver, my body was actually *aching* for him.

I'd done a lot of thinking during our time apart. I couldn't deny the feelings I had for him, but I knew I would never be able to act on them. He was my target, and pulling him into my life as a *Seductor* would kill us both. I *could*, however, embrace the time we had together. I knew the desire I had for him would help me complete my mission. Real feelings were far better than any fake emotion, but ultimately, it could only end one way.

Once I had the file from his hard drive, I would have to disappear from his life forever.

Part of me prayed I wouldn't find it here in New York...that I'd have to check his other eight properties until I did. It might even give us an entire year together. Who knew? Eventually, though, I *would* gain what I'd be assigned to steal, and for the first time since becoming a Seductor, that broke me in two.

When the plane finally touched down, I was quick to collect my bags and head toward arrivals. Oliver had insisted that I take his offer of a first class ticket for the flight, but he was already doing enough by putting me up for a week. Shy, insecure Jade wouldn't have accepted his offer, which was why I made my own flight arrangements. I did, however, agree to let Oliver meet me at the airport, so that was who I was searching for as I came out of the terminal—brown, almost black eyes that would gaze into my soul and break me apart piece-by-piece.

Three weeks apart, and the moment our eyes met, I dropped my bags and ran into his arms. Oliver lifted me off my feet as our lips crashed together furiously. I didn't need my breath; all I needed in that moment was him.

"Hi," he panted when we broke apart.

"Hi," I giggled.

"Miss me much?" he winked, motioning toward the two guys stood next to him. They immediately began to collect my bags and my cheeks flamed in embarrassment. I hadn't realized we had an audience.

"Maybe just a little," I grinned as he pulled me against him.

"I missed you, too," Oliver whispered as we made our way through the crowd.

"A limo?" I questioned when we'd made it outside.

"*My* limo," he winked.

"Are you going to put the privacy screen up?" I questioned seductively once he'd taken a seat next to me.

"You have no idea how much I wish I could, but I only have time to pick you up and drop you off at my apartment. I have an important meeting in an hour."

I pouted. "Are you this busy the entire week?"

"Only today, Beautiful," he smiled, playing with a loose strand of my hair. "I was hoping to have everything wrapped up yesterday, but the meeting ran over and well, I won't bore you with all the details. Let's just say that I sometimes do business with real assholes."

"I deal with assholes, too," I grinned, thinking back to Mr. Roswell in Rome. He was having a hard time of it lately and had to pull out of an important conference in China. That's what happened when you slept with prostitutes and everyone found out, though.

"I'm sure you do. I hope I'll be a refreshing change for you." *Oh Oliver, you are—in every single way.*

"You already are," I blushed, looking away from him while playing with the zipper on my purse.

"I want you to treat my apartment as if it were your own

while you're here," he muttered against my ear, turning my chin so I had to look at him. "I want to open up my world to you, Jade."

"Oliver, I...I..." I was mesmerized by his eyes as they burned away any defenses I'd ever had.

"You did it for me in St. Petersburg, so I want to do the same for you here. I'm a billionaire, though, so it's all on a larger scale. Just remember it's still me and don't be scared by any of it."

"Okay," I gulped, closing my eyes when his hand reached up to stroke my face.

"You're so beautiful, Jade. Christ, I want you so badly right now."

"Then have me," I pleaded, inching closer to him. My body was burning with need and desire, and I wasn't sure how much longer I could keep up with my shy, insecure Jade act.

"Don't tempt me," he said huskily. "I only have so much restraint."

"What time is your meeting again?" I muttered coyly, playing with his pale blue tie.

"An hour." He groaned, watching my lips as his hands glided toward my waist. All hesitation gone, he pulled me onto his lap as he pushed for the security screen. "Duncan, keep driving until I say otherwise," he spoke over the intercom before turning back to me. "You're becoming as insatiable as I am, Jade. Unfortunately, we can't go the entire way. I don't have any condoms."

"I'm on the pill. I'm safe. If you don't mind and you trust me, we can..." I didn't even finish my words before Oliver's mouth was hard against mine. His hands immediately slipped under my skirt and he slid my panties to the side.

"Jesus, you're so wet already," he growled against my

mouth. "Are you that desperate for me?"

"Yes," I gasped, going for his slacks that his erection was already straining against. "Enough talking, Oliver, please," I begged, thrusting into his hand. "We don't have long."

"Shit!" He pulled my panties down my legs and off while I worked on getting his cock released. He had my shirt half unbuttoned, too, by the time he was fully free. I gently rubbed him up and down and smiled against his mouth when I felt him harden even more from my touch.

"I'm going to have to make this quick. Are you ready?" Oliver groaned, throwing his head back as my drenched sex made contact with his erection. "Fuck, that feels amazing."

It was the first time I'd gone bareback with a man in a long time, but I had thoroughly read through his medical records. I knew he was clean and I was protected, and I couldn't wait to feel him pulsing inside me. Oliver was different from any target I'd ever had. I wanted to feel *all* of him without *any* barriers between us.

Taking my time to really feel him, I slowly sank down onto his length. He was cursing and gripping my hips tightly as I engulfed him in my dripping wet sex.

"Ready?" I asked when he finally looked up at me.

"Fuck, do you have idea how amazing this feels?"

"I think it's about to get much better," I grinned, rolling my hips. Oliver stilled me as his eyes became dark and hungry. His hands palmed my bra-covered breasts before pulling the cups down so he could attack my nipples and thrust up into me at the same time.

How did he do it? With the first thrust, he hit *that* spot, making me buck against him in pleasure.

"Hold on, Beautiful," he cooed into my chest, licking and sucking my nipples like he was a starving man. Then he really began to move me, lifting me up quickly by my ass before slamming me back down onto his member. It felt incredible. Arching my back, I gripped his shoulders tightly as he pounded into me over and over again. He was cursing under his breath and I knew he must have been close, because I wasn't too far away, either.

"God, I've...missed...this," Oliver mumbled between thrusts.

"Mm...so good," I moaned, losing my train of thought. That was the power this man had over me.

I began to tremble and fall down around him, but Oliver silenced my screams with a kiss as he followed soon after. When I felt him explode inside me, I bit down softly on his bottom lip and ran my hands into his hair.

"You didn't hold back," he gasped when we pulled apart slightly to gaze at each other. "I could feel you letting everything go."

"I won't be holding back anymore. I want you to have it all," I beamed, kissing him softly. Oliver snarled against my mouth, pushing me down onto the seat of the limo. His hands were instantly back in my sex.

"Oliver," I whimpered. "What about your meeting?"

"I have a few more minutes. I need to watch you come undone again. Right. Now." With that, he thrust three fingers into me over and over again, hitting places inside me that I had no idea even existed. All I could feel was him coaxing another orgasm to the surface.

I never wanted any of this to end.

"Are you going to be late for your meeting now?" I asked once we'd cleaned ourselves up with some wipes. *Who has wipes in their limo?* It made me wonder if Oliver had had a lot of limo sex before me. I wasn't sure why the thought of him with another woman enraged me so much, but it did.

He looked at his watch. "I should be okay," he smiled, stroking my face. "I wouldn't have missed *that* for anything."

"Sorry," I winced. "I have no idea what came over me."

"Don't apologize for what just happened. It was amazing. I'll be counting the minutes until I can get back to the apartment, strip you naked, and worship that amazing body of yours. I'll feed you, too, of course. Duncan will let you into my apartment while I attend my meeting. It's going to be amazing having you there waiting for me when I get home later."

"Do you need me to do anything? I could start dinner or…"

"Just rest, Beautiful. Dinner will be taken care of for us," Oliver interrupted.

"I really don't mind."

"Treat this like a vacation, Jade, and you're welcome to take a good look around my apartment." He *really* shouldn't have said that. The limo came to a stop and Oliver pouted, looking at me. "This is my stop. I'll see you later."

"Okay," I breathed against his mouth. "I can't wait to get you all to myself this afternoon." He grinned, but I could tell he was trying to compose himself as he stepped out of the limo. With a shy smile, I blew him a kiss before he walked into his office building.

It looked like New York was going to be a lot of fun.

His apartment in Manhattan was stunning and put my

place back in Florida to shame. He obviously wasn't joking about trying to see past his wealth. Oliver Kirkham was rich—I knew that—but to finally see it with my own eyes as I gazed around one of his *nine* homes was a lot to take in.

Duncan showed me into the lobby area where the elevators were. Gold-plated mirrors and black marble covered every visible surface, and I knew the apartment was going to be breathtaking if the lobby was anything to go by.

My mouth fell to the floor as Duncan showed me inside, disarming the security system. Three oversized bay windows set in large arches covered one entire wall of the living area. There were also three giant chandeliers hanging from the center of the space, and I could see a large, open kitchen in the far corner. I walked further into the huge room, noticing a large, black staircase with gold banisters that extended across the entire top floor, splitting in two directions. As I walked up the stairs, I saw that they led to the master bedroom. *Holy shit!* Oliver's master bedroom spanned the entire top floor. I couldn't even see the end of the room, but the gold, four-poster bed was *massive* and was covered in red and gold show pillows.

Did Oliver live here alone? Why would he need all this space? I couldn't even *begin* to fathom the possible reasons.

I don't know why I was freaking out so much. It wasn't as if I was going to be in his life very long. This time next year, all of this would be a fading memory. Still, it was a lot to take in.

I finally walked out onto the balcony and could see all of Central Park in the distance. I had to be at least six stories high up here, and the view was incredible. The balcony wrapped around the entire building and had comfy, brown leather outdoor couches and chairs positioned around a large glass table.

"Is there anything I can get for you, Miss Gibbs?" Duncan asked while I was standing there, still gawking at everything around me. "Mrs. Davis is out this afternoon, but she'll return later this evening."

"Mrs. Davis?" I asked in confusion.

"Mr. Kirkham's housekeeper. She lives in the staff residence on the other side of the building." Of course Oliver would have a housekeeper. The man could only cook an omelet, after all. I'm surprised he didn't have a butler, too. "I'm sure she'll come and introduce herself when she gets back. Mr. Kirkham has already informed her of your arrival."

"Thank you, Duncan," I smiled shyly.

"If that's all you need from me, I'll get back to Mr. Kirkham."

"Oh, don't let me keep you," I stressed, still taking in my surroundings. "I'm sure I'll find my way around just fine."

Duncan smiled and nodded politely before excusing himself, leaving me alone in Oliver's luxurious penthouse. Why did I feel so guilty? This was my mission—my job. It was the reason I was here in the first place.

I ran my hands over the fabric of Oliver's plush furniture as I walked back into the living room. The apartment had a renaissance feel to it, and soon my eyes fell upon the few large pieces of artwork on his walls. Some *had* to be prints. One painting was *The Tempest* by Giorgione—an interesting piece for Oliver to have. The word *tempest* could be used to describe what I did for a living. Being a Seductor meant creating uproar. I knew for a fact the original *Tempest* painting was in Venice, but it still surprised me that Oliver's taste in art was so varied.

The paintings he'd purchased in St. Petersburg were so modern compared to these, but then those pieces wouldn't have worked in this space.

I continued to wander around and found a locked door. It could have been the access to his housekeeper's living space or perhaps an office, but I'd need to work on finding out which.

After an hour or so of looking around, I decided to head back up to the master bedroom. I needed to unpack and make sure none of my clothes were too crumpled from the trip.

The bathroom was absolutely *huge!* In fact, everything in his apartment screamed wealth. I put my toiletries in a cabinet knowing Oliver wouldn't mind, and then took a better look around. The room was set in pale green marble and had a bathtub you could swim in—literally. Mirrors covered the entire back wall and were edged in gold.

I couldn't take looking around anymore—it was all too much—so I decided to lie on the giant four-poster bed and read a book. It took me five full minutes to take all the show pillows off and set them aside. Did Oliver do this every night before getting in? He was *crazy* if he did.

Oh. My. God! His bed was amazing. I'd never felt anything nearly as comfortable as I lay down, kicking my shoes off first. If I had to guess, I'd say it was memory foam. It didn't take me long to get comfy and submerge myself in my book until Oliver got back.

* * *

"Hey, Sleeping Beauty." I could hear Oliver's voice in my ear as his hand caressed my face gently. I must have fallen asleep while reading my book. "It's time to wake up. Mrs. Davis has prepared some dinner for us." I stretched with a little yawn, finally opening my eyes to see him smiling down at me. "I have to say this is the best thing I've ever come home to—you wrapped up, asleep in my bed."

"I didn't realize how tired I was," I mumbled, sitting up and trying to get my bearings. *Where the hell was I?* Oh, Oliver's apartment...that's right.

"What do you think of the place?" he asked, sitting down on the bed beside me.

"I guess I don't really mind slumming it for a week," I teased. "Seriously, though, I could get lost in here. Do you live alone?"

"Mrs. Davis lives in the staff quarters on the side of the building. She saw that you'd fallen asleep and didn't want to disturb you." Wow! Oliver *did* live here alone—that was really sad. "My father bought this apartment forty years ago, so I grew up here. I guess this would be considered my main place of residence since I spend a lot of time here compared to my other properties."

"Do *you* get lost in here?" I teased with a smile.

He chuckled, shaking his head at me before his eyes became hungry as he looked down at my mouth. "I'm so happy you're here, Jade," he whispered, leaning toward me. I licked my lips, feeling my stomach flutter in anticipation at his approach. His hand cupped the side of my face before he gently pressed his lips to mine.

Oliver always tasted of mint, and like every other kiss we'd had, it didn't take long until I'd opened my mouth so my tongue could meet with his. Desire filled me, and my arms wrapped around his neck, pulling him down onto the bed so he was on top of me.

"We should eat," he groaned, kissing down my neck while my hands clawed his back through his crisp white shirt.

"I want you, Oliver...now," I begged, arching up toward him.

"Ugh...Jade, I want you, too, but if we start, we'll never eat. You have no idea the things I want to do to you right now." I could feel a gush of wetness between my legs at his words. "And I need to introduce you to Mrs. Davis." He smirked, pulling back to find me pouting at him. "Once we've eaten, I promise we'll have *all* night." *All night*? *Mm...that sounded good to me.*

"Okay," I sighed, watching as he moved off of me. *Oh my! Someone has a problem in his pants.* "Are you going to introduce me to Mrs. Davis with that?" I questioned, motioning toward his *very* obvious erection.

He looked down at himself and then back up to me with a wink. "Oh, um...we'll give it a few moments. Mrs. Davis is an old woman. I don't want to frighten her."

"It *is* quite frightening," I teased. "I still can't believe you can get *that* inside me." I blushed on cue at my statement. Innocent Jade could be fun to play sometimes.

A playful expression crossed Oliver's face as he stalked toward me, crawling back onto the bed. "That's because I *always* get you nice and *wet* first, Beautiful," His voice was pure sex as he grabbed my legs and pulled them open. "I bet you're wet right now just from my words."

"Oh, God," I moaned, throwing my head back against the pillows.

"Mm...Jade, I can feel your dampness through your

panties," he purred, running his hands across my covered sex.

"I thought I needed to meet your housekeeper," I said breathlessly, feeling his hands slip inside my panties.

"We will. I just need to make sure I'm right first," he explained as his fingers moved into my slick folds. My hands began to scratch at the headboard behind me when he inserted two digits, rubbing the inner walls of my sex. "Mm...yes, I am. Christ, Jade, you're dripping." I really was, too. As he continued to stroke me softly, I felt more wetness gush down.

I'd always had a very high sex drive—it was the main reason I was so good at my job—but Oliver had released a whole new level of desire from within me.

"Okay," he suddenly replied, removing his fingers just as I was starting to enjoy myself.

"Are you *serious*?" I snarled, lifting my head up in annoyance. Damn it! I was breaking character again.

"You'll get more of that later, I promise. It's not helping my...*problem*," he mused, licking his fingers. Ugh, did he have to keep doing that? I smiled, looking down at the even bigger bulge in his pants.

"Well, I need to use the bathroom now—no thanks to you," I scolded, scooting off the bed. "I suggest you use that time to control your *problem*." To tease him even more, I gently cupped his erect member before darting into the bathroom. A low growl seemed to erupt from his chest as I shut the door.

CHAPTER TEN

Oliver was waiting for me when I came out of his bathroom—his *problem* barely noticeable anymore.

"Better?" he asked with a smirk.

"Just try and keep your hands to yourself while you introduce me to Mrs. Davis," I warned, raising my eyebrow at him as we made our way down the grand staircase.

"I'll try my best," he snorted from right behind me.

I could hear who I assumed was Mrs. Davis humming to herself in the large kitchen before I actually saw her. She was a mature lady with short grey hair and a warm, caring smile.

"You must be Jade." She pulled me into a tight hug, taking me by surprise. "Oliver hasn't stopped talking about you since he met you in London."

"Don't give Jade a complex, Mrs. Davis," Oliver chuckled, pulling me against his side. "I haven't been *that* bad."

"You've been bad enough," she teased, moving to turn the stove off.

"It's lovely to meet you, Mrs. Davis," I smiled shyly. "Dinner smells amazing." It really did.

"It's only homemade pizza with a side salad, but it's one of Oliver's favorite meals."

"And I imagine he washes it down with a bottle of beer," I guessed, looking over at Oliver who was gazing up at the ceiling.

"Yes, he does," Mrs. Davis laughed. "It seems you know him extremely well already."

"It seems I do," I replied. Oliver was watching me intently when my eyes met his. Did he like the fact I knew him so well already? *None of this should matter, Jade. Focus!*

"Why don't you two take a seat in the dining area? You can grab two beers on your way," Mrs. Davis suggested. "I'll tidy up in the morning to give you some space tonight."

"Thank you, Mrs. Davis," Oliver replied, taking two beers from his fridge before leading me to the table in the dining room.

"You could get a whole football team around this table," I muttered as he pulled a chair out for me. "You *are* taking the seat next to me, right? I'm not sure I'd be able to see you if you chose the seat at the end."

"Are you mocking my table?"

"No," I grinned, watching as he took the seat next to me.

"This table once belonged to King George II."

"The King of *England*?" I gasped, quickly pulling my elbows off the surface in front of me. It didn't feel right even *leaning* on a table that had once belonged to English royalty.

"Jade," Oliver chuckled, stroking my leg softly. "I don't think George II would mind if you put your elbows on the table. He's been dead since 1760."

"Funny, smart ass," I glared. "I was more concerned about how much this table costs. I'd hate to scratch it somehow."

"I scratched it several times as a child. Don't worry about it," he grinned, lost in a memory from his past. "You see those scratches there?" My eyes fell to where he was pointing. "I tried to write my name and my father went *crazy*." I found that so funny and was still laughing with Oliver when Mrs. Davis came up behind us with dinner.

"Enjoy, my dears." She smiled kindly while placing the amazing food down on the table. "I'll see the pair of you in the morning." After we both thanked her, she left without another word. I did, however, notice she didn't go through the door that had been locked earlier. It must be Oliver's office. The main hard drive could only be a matter of yards from me, so why wasn't I more excited at that prospect?

"This is amazing," I mumbled around my second mouthful of food.

"Mrs. Davis is a wonderful housekeeper," Oliver replied, sipping his beer. I was drawn to his lips, realizing that we were *finally* alone.

"How long has she worked for you?"

"All my life. She's been the mother I never had." Wow, I wasn't expecting him to say that. Oliver didn't have a mother— I knew from his file that she'd died when he was very young. Reading that information back when I'd first gotten it hadn't bothered me, but now, looking into his sorrowful, deep brown eyes, it was different.

"You didn't know your mother?" I whispered, leaning out to take his hand in mine. He shook his head but didn't say a word. "I'm so sorry, Oliver."

"It's fine, Jade. I had my father and he was amazing. He gave me everything I ever needed and spoke about her every day. I feel as if I *did* know her." That was the saddest part of Oliver Kirkham's story. Not only had he lost his mother as a baby, but his father—who'd raised him pretty much his whole life—began to show symptoms of Alzheimer's at an early age. Oliver had to take over his father's company even though he was only twenty-two at the time. He had the help of his uncle, Richard Kirkham, though, who served as his mentor. It seemed as if his father was being cared for in a nursing home in Macon, near Oliver's family residence.

"Your father sounds like an amazing man." I smiled timidly, reaching for my beer. I didn't want to push the matter, but I wanted him to feel like he could open up to me if he wanted to.

"He is." I could tell by the tone in his voice that Oliver wasn't going to say anything else, and I understood why. I'd only known him for a month or so. This was a hard topic for him because it would make him very vulnerable, and that wasn't something I was sure he would *ever* want me to see.

I helped him take the plates into the kitchen when we were done, watching as he filled his dishwasher and turned it on.

"I'm impressed," I giggled while he dried his hands. "You're more domesticated than I thought you'd be."

"I don't like to let money define me. I make sure I can still do the simple, everyday things. Having money can rot your mind if you don't keep yourself grounded."

"Those seem like wise words," I commented as he crossed the room, pulling me toward him.

"They came from a very wise man," he murmured, leaning down and capturing my lips in a deep, sensual kiss. "Come on, I want you in my bed—now."

"You don't like to waste any time, do you?" Oliver had a playful glint in his eyes, and before I could even blink, he had grabbed me and thrown me over his shoulder. I screamed, smacking his ass and demanding that he put me down, but he ignored me.

He threw me onto his bed, caveman style, and when I saw the look in his eyes I was instantly turned on.

"Mm...alone at last," he purred, unbuttoning his shirt.

"You're stripping down before me for once?" I teased.

"Yes. It means I can concentrate on you for the rest of the night," he winked, moving to unbutton his pants. In the dim light of his bedroom, Oliver's body looked even more defined than usual—the shadows caressing his skin. "Christ, I've dreamed of you lying in my bed ever since London. I can't believe you're finally here." He crawled up toward me when the only thing he still had on were his black boxers.

"I love your bed. I could quite easily stay here the entire week and not move."

"That could be arranged," he muttered, his hands running up under my skirt. "Mm...I'm trying to decide whether to strip you naked and fuck you, or fuck you now, then strip you naked and fuck you again."

"Ugh...both sound pretty damn good," I groaned, the heat flooding through me as his hand cupped my sex.

"I think I need to get you naked. I want every inch of your skin exposed to me." He certainly had a way with words, and it was causing a waterfall between my legs. "You'd like that, wouldn't you, Jade?" I could hardly speak as Oliver undid my skirt and then lifted my hips so he could pull it down my body. "You want me to worship you all night, don't you?"

"Yes!" I fisted the bedspread behind me as he slipped his hand inside my panties.

"I can feel how much you want me." *Oh, I really do!* I

pouted when he removed his fingers. He made light work of the buttons on my shirt before pulling me up and capturing my lips with his as he slipped it down my body and unhooked my bra. "Mm...now *that's* a sight," he smoldered, looking down at me as I lay before him in just my black lace panties. "I'm not sure where to start."

"Anywhere...start anywhere," I yearned, feeling his hands slowly travel up my calves. His fingertips caressed my knees and thighs before he grabbed my legs, spreading them and pulling my panties away.

"Mm...*that's* what I want," he mused, leaning down toward my sex. The moment his lips met with my slick folds, my hands entwined in his hair and my legs locked his head in place. His tongue massaged every inch of my center, and it was sending waves of pleasure throughout my body. When his fingers began to move in and out of me, I lost it, groaning out a long string of nonsensical words.

"I hope you're ready for a long night, Jade," Oliver grinned, moving up my body. When our lips met, I moaned into his mouth, tasting myself on his tongue. "You can taste yourself and you like it, don't you?" I answered by kissing him deeper, twirling my tongue frantically against his. My response only fuelled his desire, and within seconds, I felt him slip deep inside me. *Oh, now the fucking would begin.*

Oliver pulled my legs up over his shoulders and I cried out as he filled me completely.

"Shit! This feels amazing," he grunted, pausing for a second to try to compose himself. "Are you ready, Beautiful?"

"I'm always ready for you," I grinned, and with that, Oliver began to move erratically in and out of me. Never once did his eyes leave mine. It was as if he wanted to see every single emotion he was making me feel as it reflected in my eyes.

Completely lost in the pleasure, my eyes drooped when I started to climax.

"Don't...lose eye contact with me," he demanded. "I want to see you feel it all." As my orgasm built, I could feel him begin to twitch inside me. *Oh, my!* We were about to climax together. Watching Oliver come undone above me while my orgasm rippled through my body was perhaps one the most erotic things I'd ever felt. In all my years of being a Seductor, I *never* thought it could feel like this.

"Wow," I muttered when he collapsed on top of me, resting his head against my chest. "It keeps getting better."

"That's because we're learning from each other," he whispered, running his nose against my left nipple.

"You seem rather clued in on all this sex stuff," I mused, looking down at him.

"I may be well experienced, but I've never had this level of desire with anyone, Jade. I've told you this before."

"So, have you had a lot of um...lovers?"

He looked up at me from his place on my chest. "Why do you ask?"

"You're a very handsome man, Oliver. And let's not forget the fact that you're rich. I'm not stupid. I know what a catch you are."

"But you're not after my money," he cooed, moving to suckle on my right breast. *No, I was after something far worse.*

"Are you deliberately trying to avoid my question?" I asked, running my hands through his hair while fighting to control my moans of pleasure.

"What question?" he teased, burying his face back into my chest. He wasn't getting away with it that easily, though.

"You can tell I haven't had many partners," I lied innocently. I knew for a fact my number would probably be *double* his. "It doesn't have to be exact—just a rough number."

"Why does it matter? My previous partners were nothing compared to you." Damn, he really *was* trying to avoid the question.

"It's *a lot* then," I sighed. I moved to sit up but Oliver held me down.

"It's not as many as you think," he stressed. "I don't sleep around, Jade. I can't afford to in my line of business."

"What does that even mean? I think you're just making excuses!" I snapped, finally pulling out of his grip.

"It's not even fifty, okay?" he called back from where I left him on the bed. Wow, I thought it might have been at least a hundred.

"That's still a lot to me," I muttered, taking his shirt and slipping into it.

"Aren't you coming back to bed?" Oliver frowned when I began doing up the buttons.

"I need a cup of coffee first," I smiled timidly. "Do you want one?"

"Coffee in between sex—I think you're stalling," he mused, resting his arms behind his head. His aroused, naked form made me lick my lips. Christ, he was stunning...every inch of him, from his well-defined six-pack to the nicely-formed V shape where his lower abs met his hip flexors. Yeah, I knew the human body pretty well; one of my many masks as a Seductor was a fitness instructor. Oliver had to work out, but when? I'd never seen him do any exercise. "I don't think you want coffee right now, Jade," he cooed, breaking me from...well, eye fucking his naked body.

"What do you think I want instead?" I squirmed, looking down the stairs. When I turned back, he was gripping his full erection, gazing hungrily at me.

"I think you want this, Beautiful," he rasped, stroking himself up and down. Fuck, he looked so sexy doing that, and he was right—I *did* want him. "Why don't you come back to bed and take it?" How could I resist that offer?

I crawled up the bed with a sly smirk, still wearing his shirt. Having hardly buttoned any of the buttons, I knew he would be able to see parts of my breasts from this angle.

When my hand gently stroked his erection, Oliver threw his head back and groaned. I wanted to suck him until he exploded in my mouth, but shy Jade would have difficulty with that. It didn't mean that I couldn't taste him and twirl my tongue around a few times before I rode his hard length, though. Just the thought of that had me clenching my legs together.

"Whoa, Jade," Oliver gasped when I licked the tip of his length. "You don't...fuck...you don't have to do that."

"I just want a taste," I pouted, looking up at him through my long lashes while I licked down the base of his throbbing member. It worked; not only did Oliver grow harder, but he also moaned, throwing his head back onto the pillow. *Mm...someone can't watch me because they are afraid of cumming in my mouth instantly.* If only I could show him how wild I could be. I knew *several* ways of making him cum almost instantly.

As much as it pained me to do so, I pushed those ideas to the back of my mind. This was shy Jade, after all. She would blush at some of the things I could do. I used my one hand to stroke Oliver's length up and down while I ran my tongue over every inch of him. His salty essence had me humming around him in satisfaction.

"Fuck, Jade! Baby...you feel *so* good." *Baby?* Wow! I *was* driving him crazy.

"I'm not sure I can, you know—make you cum like this," I muttered, removing my mouth from him.

"You don't have to do anything you don't want to." He smiled sincerely as he opened his arms for me, and when he did, I moved so I was straddling his hips. "Mm...this won't do," he mused, undoing my top. "That's better." I giggled down at him as his hands cupped my breasts. "Are you going to lead this one?" I nodded, chewing on my lip as Oliver helped guide me down onto his length. I took him in slowly, squeezing against the intrusion. "Shit...yeah...that's it," he grunted as I began to rock against him. I took it slowly. I couldn't blame the alcohol this time if I went all 'hell cat' on him. It was a slower build this time, but with all the soft kisses and caresses he gave me while I led us to our climaxes, I was glad I took my time. When we did finally orgasm, it was almost as one.

We fell asleep after that, wrapped up in each other's arms. One thing I did know—sex had *never* felt like that before. Something deep inside me was telling me that it wasn't just sex anymore, and that thought both terrified and thrilled me.

* * *

I awoke the next morning to find the bed beside me empty. Oliver was clearly an early riser. Mm... *Get your mind out of the gutter, Jade!* I'd only just woken up; how could I be thinking about sex already?

After pulling on my sweats and a T-shirt, I brushed my hair and wrapped it up into a bun, then headed downstairs to find him.

Mrs. Davis was humming to the radio in the kitchen when I got there. *Oh. My. God!* Were those pancakes I smelt?

"Good morning, Mrs. Davis," I called, making her jump. She spun around to face me while clutching her chest. "Oh, I'm sorry if I startled you," I apologized shamefully.

"Sorry, my dear. It isn't your fault, I'm just not used to having company this early in the morning. Oliver is always at the gym until seven." That explained a lot.

"Is his gym nearby?" I asked, taking a seat at one of the kitchen stools.

"In the basement of this building. Oliver has a stake in it." That didn't surprise me. "Would you like some coffee?"

"Please," I beamed.

"Oliver likes fresh coffee in the morning. It's the first thing I do when I get up. Plus, there is no better smell to wake up to than freshly ground coffee." I couldn't agree more. "How do you take it?"

"White with one sugar, please."

"*Sugar?*" Mrs. Davis frowned. "You seem sweet enough." Yeah, if only she knew the truth. I sniggered to myself, looking toward the front door as it opened.

Holy shit! Hot, topless, sweaty, sexy Oliver had just gotten back from his workout. Did I mention he was topless?

I was mesmerized as I watched the beads of sweat trickle down his pecs. If Mrs. Davis hadn't been standing right next to me, I might have been tempted to run my tongue up and down his chest.

"Good workout?" I asked as Mrs. Davis touched my shoulder, handing me a cup of freshly brewed coffee.

"You're awake," Oliver grinned, wiping himself down with his towel.

"I must have felt you leave," I muttered into my cup. "How often do you use the gym?"

"Every morning except Sundays," he replied. Damn, that explained the fuck-hot body.

"I've made pancakes with fruit for breakfast. Is that okay with both of you?" Mrs. Davis asked, wiping her hands on her apron.

"It smells delicious," I replied, feeling Oliver's hand as he placed it softly in the small of my back. It wasn't a sexual touch; it was more loving.

"Well, Oliver, go have your shower. It will be ready in ten minutes."

"That's me being told," he chuckled in my ear. After a quick kiss to my cheek, he dashed upstairs.

"You seem to be really good for him, Jade," Mrs. Davis called from her place at the stove. "I haven't seen him this happy in a long time." I wanted to be happy with that bit of information, but I knew that in a few months—maybe even less—I would be breaking his heart.

"He's an amazing man, Mrs. Davis. I like him a lot."

"I can see that, my dear." She smiled genuinely over her shoulder at me. "Oliver is very taken with you, too."

"It was kind of an instant attraction thing in London," I mumbled, fidgeting with my cup.

"These things often are, but it would seem the two of you were meant to be. Oliver doesn't open his home to just anyone. In fact, you are only the second woman he has ever brought here to meet me." Instantly, I wanted to know who the first woman had been. "He has always been so driven by his job that I worried life might pass him by. Now I'm not so worried." She winked at me just as I heard footsteps coming down the stairs.

Oliver came into view, wearing black pants and a pale blue shirt and looking very casual.

"What are our plans for today, then?" I asked excitedly as we sat at the table eating breakfast.

"I thought I'd take you out for lunch and then maybe go and watch a show tonight."

"A show?"

"Yeah, I was thinking about the Opera or a Broadway show. It's up to you."

"Um…I'm not really sure what's playing at the moment."

"We could just stay in if you wanted to," Oliver winked suggestively.

"Maybe we should go out so I can have a short reprieve," I sniggered.

"I just want one day with you, Jade. We haven't seen each other for three weeks and I've missed you." How did he manage to make my heart swell like that? This was all so wrong and I knew it, but a large part of me adored every word he spoke.

"As long as we start to redesign your office," I teased. "That's why I'm here, after all."

"We can start that tomorrow. My uncle is in the office today, and I want to introduce you to him. We can at least stop by and have a look around while we're there." Christ, I would be meeting the family already. I needed to get myself in gear and finish this mission before I got in too deep.

"Oh, okay," I gulped.

"That's okay, isn't it, Jade? I told you about Richard, my uncle. He's also my lawyer." Now that he had mentioned it, I did remember him saying something about that the last time we were together. Of course, I already knew everything about Oliver's life before we ever even met. "I have a few things to do in my office here first, which I can do while you get ready." I nodded, swallowing my last piece of pancake.

Oliver was going to his office—it seemed as if I had some work to do once I'd gotten ready to go out.

CHAPTER ELEVEN

Once I'd had my shower, I pulled a tight, black, mid-length skirt from my suitcase. I needed to try and gain access to Oliver's computer while he was in his office, and I knew of one way I might be able to do that. After digging around for a minute, I found my thigh highs and the new pink blouse I'd purchased last week. I needed to distract Oliver while I searched his computer, and I had a feeling my plan was going to work perfectly.

"You look lovely, my dear," Mrs. Davis called. She was putting her coat on as I made my way down the grand staircase. I had gone all out, curling my hair and applying my makeup so I had sexy, smokey eyes. "I'm heading out to buy some groceries. Is there anything you need?"

"No thank you," I beamed, quickly glancing over to see that the office door was still open. Mrs. Davis nodded and then shouted goodbye to Oliver before she headed out.

"I hope I'm not intruding," I said, peeking around the door. He was frowning at his computer screen until he looked up at me.

"Wow! You look amazing," he gasped, swallowing hard as his eyes raked over my body.

"I wasn't sure what to wear, so I went for the

sophisticated, casual look."

"If this is your casual look, then I can't wait to see what you wear when you go all glamorous," he mused, pushing his chair back as I walked toward him.

"I don't go to many glamorous events."

"That was before you met me," he muttered, watching me move to sit on his desk. I knew the slit in my skirt would show the lace of my thigh highs as soon as I crossed my legs.

"Oh, you think I'll go to all these events with you now, do you?" I teased, leaning back on my hands before crossing my legs.

Just like I knew he would, Oliver's eyes zeroed in on my thighs.

"Jesus Christ!" he snarled, moving his paperwork to the side before sliding me across his desk. "You're wearing *thigh highs*?"

"Is that a problem?" I asked innocently, sitting directly in front of him. I uncrossed my legs and parted them slightly, knowing it would drive him crazy.

Oliver ran his hands up my thighs, grabbing me roughly under my skirt. "Do you have any idea how sexy you are?"

"Sexy?" I giggled, rolling my eyes at him.

"You can't see it, can you?"

"If I was sexy, you'd have thrown me over your desk by now to have your wicked way with me," I pointed out, hoping he'd take the bait.

Oliver's eyes darkened instantly, and in one swift motion, he pulled me off his desk before turning me around and slamming me back down. Shit, it was hot! I looked up slightly, noticing that his computer was on. My plan was working perfectly.

"You mean like this?" Oliver purred into my ear, pulling my skirt up around my hips. His hands caressed my ass before quickly diving into my sex. "Fuck, you're so ready for me. Is this what you wanted, Jade—for me to fuck you on my desk?"

"Yes," I groaned, feeling him start to work me with his fingers.

"This is going to be rough. Do you have any idea how hot you look right now?" I moaned in response, gripping his desk tightly. Oliver had to get lost in the moment so I could try to check his computer. I knew I had my work cut out for me in trying not to not succumb to his sexual powers, but I needed to make it look as if I was under his spell completely. *Yeah, sometimes this job could be tough.*

With a low growl, he ripped my panties from my body, ruining them just like I'd expected. I glanced up at his screen, moaning as he cupped my sex. Stretching my hands out in front of me to make it look as if I had lost control, I pressed a button on his keyboard.

All of his documents appeared in alphabetical order, and I started to look through them. I already knew the filename that I was looking for, and if *this* was the main hard drive, the file would be here.

"Shit, you feel amazing," he cooed, rubbing my clit roughly. I looked over my shoulder at him, rolling my ass against his erection that he'd already freed from his pants. "Fuck!" Oliver grabbed my hips roughly, and with one swift thrust, he was inside me.

I groaned into the table. Fuck, he felt so good. *Focus, Jade! You can't get lost this time. You have work to do.* I could hear Sonia's voice inside my head, and that freaked the shit and the desire right out of me. She was right, too—I did need to focus.

"Oh...yes," I yearned, running my nails down his desk. "Deeper, Oliver, take me deeper...please." He pulled my hips higher as he slammed into me harder, hitting *that* spot. *Holy crap*, this was going to be impossible. I tried to lift my head up to read the file names, but the feelings he was creating inside me were too intense. I could hardly keep my eyes open. This man was *incredible*.

"Give it up, Jade. I can feel you holding it in. You promised you weren't going to hold back anymore," Oliver snarled, rubbing my clit as he thrust over and over again. "I want to watch you cum all over my desk."

"It's too much...Oliver," I panted. "I...I...fuck!" I shouted, feeling my climax begin to burn deep within me. *Fine, I'll cum just this once and* then *look at the files*. That's what I told myself, anyway. The problem was whether or not I believed it.

"That's it, Beautiful," he soothed, coaxing me through my orgasm as it shot throughout my body.

I couldn't physically move; my body was a pile of mush. With my head resting on his desk, I struggled to catch my breath. My ass was high up in the air and Oliver was slowly thrusting in and out of me as I tried to catch my breath. The wetness from my sex began dripping down my inner thighs; I was completely drenched and so turned on that I could barely move.

"Oh, you want more, don't you, Jade?" How the *hell* did he know that?

"Mm..." It was all I could mumble while I was face down on his desk.

"If you want it—you've got it." Oliver began his attack

again, rolling his hips with each thrust. I knew I had to look up this time because I wasn't sure how many more chances I'd have.

Lifting my head from the desk, I tried to focus on the screen while he continued to move. On the side of caution, I quickly glanced over my shoulder to find him watching my ass. *He was such a guy.* What was it about men and their fascination in watching their cock slide in and out of a woman's sex? Not that I was complaining; it gave me time to scroll down the list of his files. The filenames were all a single letter followed by an eight digit number sequence, and I had the specific code for the required file ingrained in my head. *Damn it!* The one I needed wasn't on the list. It wasn't the right hard drive.

I gripped Oliver's keyboard tightly as he thrust deeper inside me. Christ, I was going to cum again. This time, however, he came right behind me.

"I'm never going to be able to look at my desk in the same way, Jade," he murmured against my back a few moments later. "I better take you out for the day, though, before I want you again."

"Maybe that's a good idea. I don't want to get *too* sore."

"I didn't hurt you, did I?" he soothed, running his hands down my back before pulling my skirt back down.

"No, but I think you've wrinkled my blouse and ruined my panties," I teased.

Oliver gave me a wicked smile before pressing his lips hard against mine. "I think that was worth a wrinkled shirt and ruined panties, don't you?"

"Yes," I gasped, trying to catch my breath.

"Next time, I'll push everything off my desk and fuck you *on* it." I had to hold my legs together at his words. "But then, maybe I'll do that in Macon instead. My desk there is *much* bigger."

"Macon?" I frowned.

"My family home," Oliver commented. "It's my central point to, well…everything." Was he telling me what I thought he was? Could it really be that easy—that he would simply *give* me my answers?

"You do realize I have no idea what you're talking about, don't you?" I played my cover well, sitting up and glancing at my hair in his mirror. "Oliver, you messed my hair up," I pouted, trying to readjust my curls.

"It was still worth it and you know it," he smoldered, pecking my lips. "My mansion in Macon is near the main hub for *Kirkham Industries*. My Uncle Richard lives there with his wife and…my father." Oliver's father lived in his family home and *not* in a care home? I hadn't read *that* in his file. "He has his own annex there because…he's not well."

"Oh, Oliver," I whimpered, touching his hand softly. "It's nothing too serious, I hope."

"It's not something I find easy to talk about, Jade." He looked uncomfortable as he spoke, and I didn't blame him.

"You don't have to talk about anything if you don't want to."

"I know that, but well, my father's illness…it's kind of easier for me just to *show* you."

"How would you do that?" I asked in confusion.

"I'd take you to meet him. You'll understand then, Jade."

"You want me to *meet* your father?" I gasped. Oliver looked up at me with wide, hopeful eyes. *Oh fuck, what the* hell *was I doing?* I was going to break this man in two if I continued playing him the way I was. I couldn't stop, though—not since I was so close to completing my mission.

"Yes, Jade," he whispered, gently caressing my face with his palm while running his thumb across my lips, "I do."

* * *

"You keep fidgeting," Oliver observed. I was nervous for the first time since taking this mission. We were at *Kirkham Industries'* main office, traveling in Oliver's personal elevator, and I was about to meet a member of his family—his uncle, Richard Kirkham.

"I'm a little nervous," I admitted, glancing at my reflection in the mirrored doors.

"Why?"

"You said I was meeting your uncle, remember?"

"There's no need to be nervous about that. My uncle is a very charming man."

"Mm...it must run in the family then," I muttered with a slight smirk as the elevator doors opened.

"Well, I can't argue with that," he chuckled, putting an arm around my waist and guiding me down the hallway.

People stopped to gawk at us as we passed their offices. A flood of faces greeted him much like the time we first met in London, and just like that night, he hardly acknowledged them. His eyes were firmly fixed on me.

"You're really nervous, aren't you?" he whispered, squeezing my waist reassuringly. "You have nothing to worry about, Beautiful." If only that were true. With the information I'd gathered from Oliver earlier, I knew it might only be a matter of weeks before I completed my mission. That was why the emotions on my face were so easy to read.

Oliver stopped outside a large black door, knocking once before walking in.

"I hope we're not intruding, Uncle," he called as my eyes fell on a thin, well-dressed man sitting behind his desk. He looked tired, and I could only assume it was because the job was wearing on him.

"How could you intrude? This is your company," Oliver's uncle pointed out, looking up at us. "Ah, you must be Jade." I blushed as he got up from behind his desk to greet me. "Oliver has hardly stopped talking about you since he met you in London."

"It's a pleasure to meet you," I greeted with a smile as he shook my hand.

"I've heard you're going to brighten up Oliver's office down the hall. It's been in need of that ever since he took over from his father."

"The office isn't that bad," Oliver grumbled right before someone spoke from behind him.

"Oh, I'm sorry Oliver. I didn't realize you would be in today." A beautiful, tanned female with long brown, almost black hair, gasped when she noticed him.

"Don't mind us, Abigail," he said, smiling warmly as jealousy shot through me. *She* was the sort of woman he hired? I was beginning to understand why he was so good in bed. I could just imagine all the late night activities that had gone on behind closed doors in these offices. What I didn't understand was why I was so angry at that thought. "Miss Gibbs and I only stopped by to begin planning the remodel of my office."

"It's just that I have Mr. Franklin on the telephone for you, Richard," Abigail replied, looking at Oliver's uncle.

"Jade and I will leave you to it, Uncle. You'll stop by my apartment later, won't you? Before you fly home?" Richard nodded as Oliver pulled me toward him. Abigail watched us leave, and I couldn't help but put my hand on his back possessively. *Holy crap!* The whole situation was new to me. Jade Phillips, marking her territory with a *man.* What the hell was wrong with me?

"It was nice to meet you, Miss Gibbs." Abigail smiled sweetly as we passed her, and I couldn't help but hate the woman even more. She seemed so innocent—much like the character I had been playing since I'd met Oliver. Why couldn't he have fallen for her instead? Sweet, pure Abigail would never break his heart.

"What was all that?" he whispered in my ear as we wandered down the hallway. *Damn it!*

"What?" I frowned.

"Oh, you *know* what, Jade," he chuckled, showing me into his office. It was a lot like his apartment—very art deco, with a large, dark wood desk and deep red walls.

"Wow, you weren't kidding about needing my help in here, were you?" I teased.

"Stop trying to change the subject."

"I'm not," I frowned.

"The looks you were giving Abigail?"

"What looks?" I asked, trying to play dumb.

"Abigail is an employee, Jade. I've never pursued *any* of my employees. It's not my style." He pulled me into his chest and held me there. "And if you haven't worked it out yet, I'm too taken with you to even look at or want anyone else."

I placed my hand on his chest, playing with the buttons on his jacket as I spoke. "Was I really that obvious?" I cringed when I looked up at him, nervous of his reaction.

"Just a little," he grinned, pecking my lips. "And it was adorable."

"I don't usually get so possessive," I admitted, shaking my head. "I have no idea what came over me."

"I would have reacted the same way. Don't worry about it," Oliver soothed as he rubbed my shoulders. "And wait a minute... did I just hear you dissing my office a moment ago?"

"You're the one who asked for my help, remember? If you want to leave it this way, that's fine by me," I giggled.

"What would you do in here?"

"I think red is a very dark color for an office. You need something lighter—more calming."

"Good idea," he mused, walking to his desk and pulling me with him. "Why don't you show me some ideas online?" Taking the seat behind Oliver's desk, I watched as he leaned over me to start up his computer. I swallowed hard when he typed in his password right in front of me. *Oh. My. God*! I had Oliver's password for his New York computer. Using the decoder might not even be necessary when I got to his computer in Macon. His password for this computer was his father's name and date of birth—something I wasn't expecting. "I shouldn't really let you watch while I access my files, but I trust you," he muttered, clicking on a tab for me to use.

"I wasn't really paying attention," I lied, feeling as if my entire world was collapsing around me. This was all happening too fast. I had a possible location for the hard drive and now I had a password. I also had a feeling that Oliver used the same password for all his computers. I didn't want this mission to end, though—I wasn't ready to say goodbye to him yet.

"I have a terrible memory so I keep it simple. I use a loved one's name and date of birth," he beamed, leaning against his desk while I pulled up a few design pages for us to look at.

"Should you really be telling me this?" I laughed nervously, tucking my hair behind my ears.

"Jade, I know who I can and can't trust," he chuckled. *No, Oliver, you don't.*

"Well, it's not like you use the same password for all your files," I snickered, scrolling down the webpage of a new designer I'd heard about.

"Actually I do," he snorted.

"That's ridiculous!" I snapped, looking up at him. "If you're half as important as I think you are, that's got to be extremely dangerous?" I was so *angry* with him. How could he be so gullible? Why did Oliver have to fall for my charade so easily?

"It's not dangerous when you only tell certain people."

"Oliver, you hardly know me," I stressed, refusing to meet his gaze.

"I think I know you pretty well, Jade." I could feel his eyes on me as he spoke. "I know you're fighting with yourself—between the woman you think you *should* be and the woman you *want* to be." How did he know that? "I can feel the *real* you when I make love to you. You love the excitement, but feel guilty about wanting it, don't you?"

"I'm not as easy to read as you think I am, Oliver," I sighed, finally looking up at him.

"Does this have anything to do with your ex, Mario?" I

tried not to grimace at the mere thought. *Mario as my ex? Yuck.*

"Mario...isn't an easy subject for me." I wasn't thinking about Mario as I spoke. I did have a subject I struggled to talk about—a past I kept hidden away—but I wouldn't let that surface now. It was too painful when I thought about what I had lost.

"I can understand difficult subjects. I won't press for more until you're ready, I promise." Oliver stretched, leaning over me to look at the computer. "How about you show me some ideas for my office, instead?" That seemed like a good idea. I didn't want the conversation getting too serious, after all.

✻ ✻ ✻

"How are you finding New York, Jade?" Richard asked, sipping his whiskey while we sat on Oliver's balcony.

"It's amazing," I replied, watching Oliver make his way back toward me.

"Jade has been to New York before, Richard." I hid my laugh when Oliver shook his head, rolling his eyes.

"But I doubt she has ever seen New York from a billionaire's perspective," Richard mused, watching me intently.

"What are you trying to imply, Uncle?" Oliver suddenly spat.

"Oliver, I...I wasn't..." Richard tried to defend himself but Oliver continued.

"Why do you always have to try and see the worst in everyone? You've seen how happy Jade makes me. Not every woman who shows interest in me is after the same thing."

"Oliver..." I tried to calm him with my tone and pleading

eyes.

"You'll have to excuse my nephew," Richard replied, looking at me. "He thinks I'm overly critical of everyone he dates, but it's my job. I have the business to think about, as well as Oliver himself. I meant you no disrespect, Miss Gibbs."

"There was none taken, Richard." I smiled at him before glaring at Oliver. "I think you should apologize to your uncle for your outburst."

Richard laughed loudly. "Oliver, I like this one. I think she might be a keeper," he replied, nudging me playfully.

Oliver's face softened as he watched me. "So do I, Uncle," he admitted, taking a sip of his beer. "So do I." All I could do was gulp, my mouth suddenly very dry.

Jade, what the hell are you doing?

CHAPTER TWELVE

I didn't get much work done during my week with Oliver. Well, my interior design work, anyway. Oliver insisted on winning and dining me, taking me to art galleries, and to see a show or two. Needless to say, I was exhausted by the end of the week. I'd been able to analyze all his computers during my stay but had found nothing. The hard drive had to be in Macon.

"This week has been amazing, Jade," he cooed as he held me against his chest while we lay in his bed. "I can't believe it's our last morning together."

"You're making it sound like we're never going to see each other again," I teased, running my fingertips down his naked chest.

"I have a busy schedule these next few weeks. It's going to feel like a lifetime until I see you again."

"I'm sure you'll be far too busy to think about me."

"You'd think that, wouldn't you, considering the business that I run? But I know for a fact that I won't be able to get you off my mind." I couldn't answer him. "You know that, right?"

"I do," I sighed, still guarding my feelings. I knew he wanted me to be more open with him, but truthfully, I didn't want to hurt him anymore than I had to. I was going to break his heart in the end—there was no other way around it.

Oliver sighed deeply. "You know how I feel about you, Jade. I've made it clear from day one, yet you still seem so guarded with your feelings for me. The only time I've seen any sort of reaction from you was when you got jealous of Abigail."

"Are we really going to do the heavy stuff now? I leave in a few hours." I raised my eyebrow in question, resting my chin on my hand.

"You don't want to talk about where *this* is going?" *No, Oliver, I don't, because I know this isn't going anywhere.*

"You don't think it's still a little early? I thought we were just having fun—you know…enjoying each other's company. "

"Why do I get the feeling there is more you're not telling me?"

"I really like you. You know that, Oliver, but I have to admit, you're not my usual type."

"What do you mean by that?" he gasped, his eyes full of worry.

"You're wealth, mainly," I pointed out as if it were obvious. "Come on. You really think I'm *used* to all this?" I waved my hands at the splendor surrounding us.

"I'm not my wealth, Jade. What you've seen is the real me. Please don't be afraid of your feelings because of how rich I am."

"I just can't rush this, Oliver. I need to be careful."

"I'd never hurt you," he muttered, skimming his nose against the nape of my neck. I had to hold my legs together to keep from squirming; Oliver knew my neck was my most erogenous zone. The powers this man had when it came to my body scared the crap out of me. "I'm not like your ex."

"Why would you think this has anything to do with my

ex?" I gasped, feeling him gently bite down on my neck.

"You're really trying to tell me it doesn't?" Oliver questioned, pushing me onto my back and running his hands down my body. "You forget—I know you pretty well already."

"You know how to work my body. I'm a little more guarded with my mind." I squirmed as his hands began to wander between my legs.

"I want your mind, too," he smoldered, teasing my entrance with soft, gentle strokes. "And I'll wait as long as it takes for you to trust me with it." I couldn't respond; I was panting too much. "But, right now, I think I'll have your body again."

Everything else became insignificant then...my job—the real reason I was here—and the fact that our next meeting could be our last. Oliver had a way of making me forget the reason I was really here.

"Let it go, Jade," he whispered, rotating his fingers inside me. He was brushing against *that* spot, but not enough to make me feel the euphoria begin to build. *Oh, he was teasing me.* Mm... I could play along with that. I knew I would be having an earth shattering orgasm at the end of it, after all.

"That's it, Beautiful," he cooed, moving toward my chest. When his tongue licked over my hardened nipple at the same time he stroked my G-spot, I closed my eyes tightly and savored his touch. "Mm...Jade, you have no idea how good it feels when you give yourself to me." I grabbed his hair tightly as he began to make his way down my body, leaving a trail of hot bites and kisses.

"Oh...Oliver." My voice was just a soft whisper as his mouth made contact with my sex. I could feel his breath on me, and without warning, he thrust his tongue inside my sex. Oh, the things this man could do with his tongue. Worried that I'd pull his hair out while he continued his ministrations, I moved my hands, fisting the pillows behind me instead. When he bit down on my clit moments later, I exploded around him.

"Mm...you taste sweeter today," he mumbled, licking his way back up my body. I was still in a state of bliss, and I knew Oliver was far from finished with me. "Do you want to taste yourself, Beautiful?" We were face to face now. I answered him with a deep, passionate kiss, sweeping my tongue around his... tasting myself. *Fuck, it was hot!*

"Mm...I do taste sweet today," I giggled, licking across his bottom lip.

"You're always sweet," he beamed, positioning himself in between my legs. "It's one of the many things I love about you." Did he just mention the 'L' word? *Breathe, Jade! Just breathe.*

Nothing more was said after that. Oliver simply thrust deep inside me, taking me at a soft and loving pace.

* * *

"You'll call me when you land, right?" he asked, standing in his kitchen and looking a little lost. Mrs. Davis had just left, saying her goodbyes to me before she did.

"Of course I will," I grinned.

"Are you sure you don't want me to come to the airport with you?"

"You're letting Duncan take me. I'll be fine."

"What about payment for your services?" he smirked. Oliver knew damn well we hadn't gotten any work done when it came to redesigning his office.

"I'll get my office to send an invoice."

"You'll need to send those design prints over, too."

"I'll have to make something up," I grinned, watching as he pushed off the kitchen counter and stalked toward me. "You do realize we hardly came to any decisions regarding your office, right?"

"We decided on a calming color, and I'd like to use those paintings we brought in St. Petersburg," he teased, his hands snaking down my back.

"I guess that's a start," I giggled, wrapping my arms around his neck.

"I'd still pay the invoice, even if we hadn't gotten *any* work done. This week has been incredible, Jade."

"Thank you for letting me into your world."

"Now that you're in it, I'm not sure if I ever want you to leave," he murmured before sweetly kissing my lips. "Have a safe trip."

"I will," I breathed as Duncan came into view, collecting my bags. "You'll call me when you finally get some free time, won't you?"

"I promise," he sighed deeply.

"Okay." I took a deep, calming breath. "I'll leave you to run your empire for a few weeks."

"Thanks." Oliver's eyes looked sad as he gazed at me, and I had a sudden urge to make him feel better.

"I'll only be a phone call away. You can call me anytime," I soothed, leaning up to peck his lips. "Not that I know anything about machines or how to run an empire, but I'm still here for you."

"You don't know how good that sounds. I love my business and the people in it, but being with you—talking to you—it's the only time I feel as if I can escape."

"I love spending time with you, too," I whispered into his neck. I couldn't look him in the eyes because I knew that wasn't shy Jade talking; it was the real me.

"Get out of here before I make you stay," he said with a wink. I kissed his lips one last time, his arms still wrapped tightly around my waist and holding me to him for a few moments before finally letting me go. "I'm missing you already," he called once I reached his door. "Look after her, Duncan."

"I will, Sir," Duncan replied, leading the way to the car.

And just like that, my time in New York with Oliver was over.

* * *

"Sonia is ready to see you now, Jade," Drew winked, walking out of her office.

I frowned, shocked at seeing him. "I thought you were supposed to be in Texas?"

"My mission went bust."

"Oh no!" I gasped. I liked Drew; he was probably my favorite male Seductor. He had a thin build but was muscular, with rockstar style, mousy blonde hair and baby blue eyes. He was quite protective of me, but in a brotherly way. We'd never overstepped that mark when it came to our friendship, and he was the only other person aside from Molly and Georgie who I really felt I could talk to here.

"It wasn't my fault. The client's payment fell through."

That was the only time a target would get lucky—when a client couldn't pay the agreed price before the steal was made.

"Is Sonia giving them hell?" I chuckled.

"I think it's worse than hell," Drew snorted, running his hands through his hair.

"How long were you on the job?" I knew I couldn't go into details about a mission, but time scales were fine.

"Two months," he sighed.

"That sucks—all that work for nothing."

"It happens," he shrugged. "What about you, Jelly Bean? I've heard you have 'the' mission at the moment." I had no idea where Drew's nickname for me came from, but it always made me smile. Georgie used it all the time, as well, and I constantly gave her crap for hanging out with him too much. "How's it all going?"

"Good thanks," I grinned.

"Is that all I'm getting?" he pouted.

"You know the rules," I winked, walking into Sonia's office. "I'll meet you by the pool in half an hour. I feel like we haven't talked in ages."

"Okay, Jelly Bean. Georgie is already out there somewhere, so I'll make us all some iced tea," Drew called just before I closed Sonia's office door.

"Jade," Sonia greeted from behind her desk. "How was New York?"

"Very informative," I grinned, taking a seat in front of her.

"Do you have information on the hard drive?"

"It's in his family home in Macon."

"You know this for sure?"

"Yes. I checked his files in New York, but the hard drive

wasn't there. It will either be at his family home or the Kirkham factory nearby. Oliver practically told me that in a conversation we had."

"When will your next contact with Mr. Kirkham be?"

"He has work obligations for the next few weeks, but he won't be able to stay away from me for too long. He's already asked me to meet his father in Macon when we see each other again."

"I'm impressed, Jade. I wasn't expecting this deal to be sealed so quickly."

"I still have the hard drive to find and a password to decode, Sonia. It's not quite sealed yet."

"I have every faith in you. Stop by Intelligence before you go. They may have a few new toys for you to play with. You'll need a new tracker, too. The software has been updated." I nodded, starting to get up. "You'll get a good bonus from this mission when it's over. Our client has already paid for the steal and is very eager to get their hands on the file with the blueprints."

"This client—do you know who they are?" I knew she did. A client could only chose to remain anonymous to the Seductor, not to the organization itself.

"Why do you ask?"

"You do know what it could mean if the weapon gets into the wrong hands, don't you?"

"That isn't any of our concern. You know we check the safety of each mission before we accept the contract. We have nothing to worry about." Yeah, the Seductors would be fine, but what about the people in which these weapons were intended for? "Since when did you have a conscience?"

"I've never been given a mission where innocent people could die before, Sonia. I'm sorry if I'm finding it all a little too much to handle."

"Jade, you can't back out of this now—the mission has already been paid for. Besides, we'll get that hard drive one way or another. If you can't obtain it, it will have to be declared a Code One, and you *know* how those end." Yes, I did—with the target dead so there would be no witnesses. *No, I couldn't live with that. Oliver would not be killed because I was too gutless to finish a mission.*

"I'll get it done, Sonia. All I'm saying is that these weapons remain secret for a reason. Oliver has kept them from certain countries as a safety measure."

"None of that is your concern, Jade," Sonia spat coldly. "Maybe if you spent less time getting to know *Oliver* and more time working on your *mission,* you wouldn't feel so guilty. This is your job. You know better than any other Seductor that you can't get attached to the targets in these missions." Was I making myself too obvious? "I suggest you use these next few weeks to re-evaluate your mission and your feelings for Mr. Kirkham before you meet him again. You need to get that hard drive before you fall any deeper."

"I'm in complete control," I replied firmly, crossing my arms.

"No, Jade, you're not, and I suggest you rectify that immediately. You may leave now. I'll email you any new developments." Sonia's words were final, and I knew I had no choice but to go.

I stormed out of the office, pushing past Mario in the

hallway.

"Whoa, don't apologize then!" Mario called after me.

"Fuck off, Mario!" I snarled over my shoulder. "I'm in no mood for your shit today."

"Stop denying this, Baby. I know you get worked up because you want me." That was it! I'd had enough of his shit.

I turned on my heel and marched back over to him. "When will you ever take the *hint*? There is a better chance of me sleeping with Drew then there will ever be with you," I spat, poking his chest with my finger.

"I think you're in denial." Mario licked his lips, looking me up and down. "Come on, Jade. You know how good we'd be together. Damn, I bet people would even pay to watch us—to learn from the experts." I was going to be sick if he kept talking.

"You are such an asshole, Mario. I wouldn't even go near you if I was offered money."

"One day we might have to work together. That would involve money."

"That will never happen. Sonia knows I would never agree."

"What is your problem with me, Jade?" he asked, grabbing my wrist roughly.

"It could have to do with the fact that you're a complete *moron* who takes more time getting ready in the morning than any of the females here, but that isn't even *close* to everything. My problem with you is that you're an attention seeking *asshole* that only ever looks out for himself!" I snarled, yanking my wrist out of his grip. "And, if you ever grab me again, I will hit your balls so hard that you'll be out of action for *months*."

"You little..."

"Is there a problem here, Jade?" Drew called from behind me, interrupting Mario mid-sentence. "Your iced tea is melting."

"No, we're done here," I glared toward Mario before storming off in the direction of the pool.

"You should ignore him, Jade. He only tries to piss you off to get a reaction from you," Drew commented as we sat down.

"What happened?" Georgie asked, taking a seat with us as she removed her sunglasses.

"Mario is pissing her off again, Gummy Bear," Drew replied. His nicknames for us always made me laugh; Molly was M&M.

"It's not just Mario," I sighed, taking a sip of my tea.

"Is it the mission?" Georgie asked in concern. "I heard about how hot your target is from Molly." Damn it! Had Molly told everyone? "You have to be careful, Jade."

"She's right, Jelly Bean," Drew replied. "It must be causing you a lot of stress. I've heard what the mission price is." Missions were never complete secrets here. It made me laugh when I thought about the rules and how many were actually broken on a daily basis. "I'll help if I can. What's wrong?"

"It's not exactly the *mission*," I sighed deeply. God, I was missing Oliver already, and I'd only left him a few days ago.

"No!" Georgie gasped. "Is it the *guy*? Molly told me something about…"

"What did she say?"

"About you finally getting the big 'O'." *Goddamn it, Molly!* "It's about time. I told you it was all about letting go," she winked.

"Jelly Bean has finally had a big 'O' from a guy without her doing all the work—WOW!" Drew was dumbfounded.

"Sonia thinks I'm getting too involved."

"Are you?" Drew asked seriously.

"What does it matter if I am? It can only end one way. I have a steal to make to complete the mission."

"Oh, Baby girl, I'm so sorry. I never thought this would happen with you. You're always so focused," Georgie pouted.

"I've tried to be, I really have, but he's made me feel things I didn't even know I could feel."

"Are you near the end of the mission?"

"I'm pretty sure the next time I visit him will be my last." I smiled sadly, fighting back the tears. *Tears? Jesus, Jade, get a damn grip!*

"You've got to suck it up. Lots of Seductors have fallen for their targets. Think back to Laura—she had to take six months off to get over it. You'll bounce back, too, though. You're one of the top Seductor here," Georgie replied. I nodded, playing idly with my glass. "This is what we chose to do, Jade. We can't afford to have a sudden change of heart. We each signed up for this, knowing we have to complete any mission given to us."

"You're not going to start to quote the rules to me, are you?" I giggled.

"If it will help, I can," she grinned.

"I know them all, too," Drew winked. "We can have a study group in my room later if you want."

"I'm good, thanks." I knew them all by heart anyway. They had been etched into my mind since the day I signed the contract. "And I know what your study groups entail, Drew," I teased.

"I have no idea what you're talking about," Drew gasped, pretending to be shocked.

"She's talking about the orgies," Georgie snorted, mocking him, too.

"Are you two offering?" he winked.

"Can we get back to Jade's problem?" Georgie pointed out. An orgy with Drew, Georgie and me was never going to happen, but I was pretty sure he was joking, regardless.

"Just be careful, Jelly Bean. Don't let your heart rule your head," she replied sadly, stroking my arm. She was right and I knew it.

I realized what I had to do, so with a heavy heart, I paid a visit to Intelligence before heading back to the penthouse. I needed to prepare myself for completing my mission and having to say goodbye to Oliver.

CHAPTER THIRTEEN

"Best out of three," Drew smirked as he pinned me to the ground. I loved defense training with him because, although he made it fun, he definitely knew his stuff. He had studied the Martial Art of Muay Thai. I was actually quite envious of him when I learned that he'd been trained by the Monks of Phuket in Thailand. He was taught physical and mental discipline, including the 'art of the eight limbs,' which was about using the combination of fists, shins, elbows, knees and feet . Defense wasn't his top skill, though. He was a charmer and could charm his way into any female's panties—outside of the Seductors. It was amazing to watch, too.

"Can you show me that break hold one more time?" I asked as he helped me up off the ground.

"You like that one, huh?" he grinned, turning me around.

"A lot of guys try to grab me from behind."

"That's because you have a very sexy ass." I elbowed him in the ribs. Drew was such a tease. "What? I was just stating a fact."

"Just show me the damn move!" I snorted, shaking my head at him.

"Okay, so imagine I'm an attacker coming from behind you. You need to break the hold as quickly as possible."

"Like this?" I commented, using my arms as leverage to

break out of his hold. Once I was free, I swept Drew's left leg out from under him, knocking him to the ground.

"Hey," he complained. "That's cheating!"

"You said best out of three."

"You're going down this time."

"Uh huh, whatever you say," I challenged with a smirk.

Drew and I were still wrestling with each other when Georgie walked in.

"Your gadgets are ready in Intelligence, Jade," she called. "What the hell are you two doing? I thought you were having defense training?"

"This is defense training," I panted, slipping out of Drew's grip as he tried to grab me again.

"Stop messing around. We all have work to do," she sighed, rolling her eyes at us.

That didn't stop us, though. I managed to sweep his leg a few moments later, but Drew pulled me down with him.

"We'll call that a draw," he snorted.

"You always cheat," I giggled, hitting his chest. "Okay, I need to get my new gadgets and then head back to the penthouse."

"Missing lover boy, are you?" Oh, he was going to get slapped if he kept on the way he was. It wasn't funny.

❋ ❋ ❋

"What are you wearing right now?" Oliver breathed over the phone later that night.

"I'm in bed, Oliver. What do you think I'm wearing," I giggled.

"Shit! You're naked, aren't you?"

"Yes," I purred, running my hands down my body. Phone sex was a lot of fun with Oliver. This was the third late night call I'd had this week.

"Are you touching yourself, Beautiful?"

"Do you want me to?" I asked breathlessly. I was so turned on as I lay waiting for his orders.

"Yes. I want you to run your hands over those perfect breasts of yours while imagining they're mine." I did as he asked, palming my breasts as I closed my eyes and thought of him. "Shit, I can hear how turned on you are, Jade. Do you want to touch yourself? I bet you're already wet for me."

"Ugh...Oliver," I moaned, so desperate to feel his touch.

"Run your hands down your body and tease yourself, Jade, just like I do." *Christ, he was dirty and hot and...oh, that feels so good.* I began playing with my clit, making soft, gentle circles. "I have my cock in my hands right now and I'm thinking of you, Beautiful—only you." All that could be heard for the next few minutes was panting and groans of pleasure from both of us. I came first, almost dropping my cell as I climaxed. Oliver grunted down the phone right after me.

"Fuck," he panted.

"Do you feel better now?" I giggled.

"I'd feel better if you were here with me."

"How's it all going?"

"I have a meeting with N.A.T.O in the morning." *Holy shit!* I sometimes forgot just how important Oliver's job was. "It's been a taxing week."

"Is there any sign of light at the end of the tunnel?"

"Missing me a little bit, are we?" I could hear a chuckle in his voice and it made me smile.

"You know I am."

"I miss you, too. I'm still trying to get things tied up, but I should have a date for us soon. I need to pay a visit to the production factory in the next few weeks, and that's near Macon, so I'm hoping we'll be able to arrange something for then."

"I hope so," I sighed, rolling onto my side.

"How's work going for you?"

"Fine. I have a few local clients to see and then a trip to Miami for a few days next week." Miami was actually a small job I was doing with Drew, but I wasn't about to mention that to Oliver.

"Do you think you'll be able to fit me into your schedule in a few weeks?"

"I have weekends off, and if I need to, I can add a Friday or a Monday to it."

"That sounds like a plan." Oliver sighed deeply. "I'll call you again in a few days. Maybe next time we can FaceTime instead. I'd love to *watch* you cum, Beautiful, as well as hear you."

"Um...I..." I tried to play the innocent approach. Shy Jade would be scared by that thought.

"If you feel uncomfortable, we'll stop. Have I ever made you do something you didn't want to do? Who knows? You might even like it." Oh, I knew I'd like it alright, but poor, shy Jade would need a little push.

"I'll try it, but don't expect it to be like some porn movie."

"You've watched *porn*, Jade?" Oliver gasped. I knew he was teasing me.

"Hasn't everyone?"

"Can I ask what kind of porn it was?"

"I could tease you and say guy-on-guy," I sniggered. "But it was a BDSM themed DVD." *Ha! Take that, Oliver.* I was willing to bet he was hard again already.

"Jesus, Jade, you're full of surprises." If only he knew how true that statement was. "So, do you um...like the idea of being tied to a bed?"

"I do," I replied, trying so hard not to laugh. I wished so badly that I could see his face right then. "I've always wondered about being spanked, too."

"Fuck, Jade, we need to end this conversation before I explode."

"Have you ever done any BDSM?"

"Not really, but if you want me to tie you to a bed and fuck you into submission, I'm willing to try that." I had no doubt that he would, either.

"Mm...that sounds like a plan," I purred.

"I better go." He spoke the words, but he really didn't sound like he meant them.

"Okay, I'll speak to you soon."

"Sweet dreams, Beautiful."

"Goodnight, Oliver."

"Answer one question for me before you hang up," he quickly said. I remained quiet, waiting to hear what he had to ask. "How wet are you right now?" I couldn't help but giggle. *Oh, Oliver, I've got you thoroughly hot and bothered, don't I?* "A man needs to know these things," he added.

"I'm completely drenched," I breathed. "Goodnight." With a giggle, I quickly hung up.

Seconds later, I got a text message from him.

Tease! xxx

I had to laugh out loud at that and sent him a quick goodnight text before finally going to sleep.

* * *

"That's them," Drew muttered into his beer as our targets walked into the bar. We'd come to Miami to steal two passcards for a laboratory here in the city.

"Are we going to do this quickly or have a few drinks first?" I asked with a smirk.

"I think we have time for some drinks first." Drew's eyes wandered over to our targets as they took a seat with a group of friends. "Let's give them a chance to get drunk before we strike."

"Are you going to sleep with yours?" I knew Drew and the answer to my own question, but decided to ask anyway. I wasn't even sure he knew *how* to complete a mission without taking his target to bed.

"Is the Pope Catholic?" he teased, checking out a waitress' ass as she walked past him.

"*Drew*," I moaned, slapping his leg, "try and focus on the mission."

"What? I was just looking," he laughed, shaking his head at me. "So, are you going to tell me about this top target or not?"

"No, I'm not," I grinned, sipping my cocktail.

"Molly said he looked really rich and was an extremely good-looking guy." I already knew all this from Georgie.

"Drew, you told me all that when we were with Georgie. And besides, Molly thinks *Mario* is a good looking guy, so she isn't the best judge. Wouldn't you agree?" I pointed out.

Drew choked on his beer before conceding. "Good point."

"And you know we can't go into details about our missions. You're getting as bad as her."

"You're different with this mission. I just couldn't quite pinpoint why exactly until I heard about your big 'O.'"

"Can we shut the fuck up about my sex life? That's all you, Molly, and Georgie have gone on about these last two weeks!" I snarled. "I took this job with you so I could get a reprieve from all that."

"And here I was thinking you wanted to spend some time with *me*."

"Can we just get on with it?" I sighed, noticing Drew's target walk up to the bar. Drew looked over his shoulder and took notice, as well.

"Can I buy you a drink, Gorgeous?" he asked when his target was standing only a few feet away from him. That was Drew, though; he always dove in head-first. "You have to be the sexiest woman I think I've *ever* seen. I won't take no for an answer."

"I...um...I..." She began to stutter, looking over at me skeptically.

"I'm his sister," I smiled, knowing she might have thought that I was *with* him or something. "Don't mind me."

"Oh, I...I'd love a drink," she giggled, and just like that, Drew was already halfway to completing his part of the mission.

It didn't take long for us to join our targets and their group of friends. Drew already had his tongue down his mark's throat before I'd even introduced myself to mine.

"Can I buy you a drink?" my target asked, scooting closer

to me as we both sat on a large, bright red couch.

"I guess it won't do any harm. My brother is a little busy, anyway," I laughed, motioning in Drew's direction.

"Yeah, it looks that way," the guy smiled. "I'm Andy." He held his hand out to me.

"Mina," I smiled, shaking his hand. I was using a different name tonight—one from my past—just for the hell of it. It was my favorite name in the world. I knew it was against the rules to go by another first name for several reasons, but it was my way of saying a silent 'fuck you' to Sonia for calling me out on my mission with Oliver.

"Would you like another cocktail, Mina?"

"Please," I replied, looking down at my phone. Damnit! Of all the times Oliver would call me, it had to be now. "If you'll excuse me," I muttered, rushing outside for some privacy.

"Hey," I stressed, answering after the fifth ring.

"Hi, Beautiful. How has your day been?" he asked.

"Good. How about yours?"

"Tiring. The assholes I do business with are ruthless."

"I can imagine." Just as I spoke, a rowdy group of females began to sing nearby.

"Jade, where the hell are you? Is that singing I can hear?"

"I'm outside at a bar right now. My colleague and I decided to have a drink once we'd finished with our client."

"Oh, okay. How about you call me when you get back to your hotel? I thought we could FaceTime." I didn't miss the suggestive tone in his voice. *Mm, someone wanted to play tonight.*

"Sure, that sounds good. I'll speak to you in a bit."

"I look forward to it," Oliver cooed before we both hung up.

Drew was ready to take his target back to the hotel a few hours later. I'd already snatched the passcard from my target's jacket when he'd gone up to buy my third drink. I didn't even have to kiss him, which was why I loved these types of jobs—jobs when it was just about the steal and I didn't have to give myself up as a way to complete the mission.

"Are you sure you wouldn't like some company tonight, Mina?" my target slurred, running his hand down the side of my leg. What was it about men and always having to try and touch a girl when she wasn't interested? Like being felt up by this idiot was going to make me want him? Stupid men.

"I just got out of a long-term relationship and I'm really not that kind of girl, but thank you for the drinks." I smiled, grabbing my coat to follow Drew and his target outside. Mine was too drunk to ask any questions or even respond, or to work out that his passkey was missing. In the morning when he figured it out, it would be too late. He was so wasted he even let his friend leave with us—some friend he was.

"I'll see you in the morning, Jelly Bean," Drew winked, pulling his target into his room when we arrived back at the hotel. I had to giggle. I loved these easy missions with Drew; he was always a blast.

I messaged headquarters, letting them know that I had one keycard and that Drew would have the other by the morning. Minutes later, I received a message back with the name of the contact that was collecting the cards from our hotel early tomorrow morning.

Once I had the necessary information, I took a long soak in the bath before slipping into bed to call Oliver. *Mm...this was going to be fun.*

"You didn't stay out long after I called you." He smiled widely over the screen when I FaceTimed him. "Holy shit, Jade. Are you in bed already?"

"I thought you had plans for this phone call," I giggled. "Oliver, some things never change. I'm still naked before you." I watched his eyes grow hungry on the screen.

"Show me, Jade," he groaned. I lifted the covers, moving my phone so Oliver could see all of me. "Fuck, you are so sexy."

"I'm not sure how good I'll be at this," I admitted, biting my lip while looking into the camera. *Oh, poor, shy Jade.*

"Jade, just seeing you naked is enough. You have no *idea* the effect you have on my body."

"Maybe you should show me," I suggested with a giggle.

"How much have you had to drink tonight?" he questioned with a frown.

"Just a few cocktails."

"Oh, drunk Jade is back. I know how fun *she* is," Oliver winked, licking his lips.

"I think it's time you got naked, too, Oliver."

"Is that an order?" he questioned with a glint in his eyes.

"It is if you want to see anymore." Oh, I loved teasing him.

"Give me a few seconds." I watched the screen go blank for a moment before I saw Oliver move over to his bed. Damn, he was such a fine sight. I wanted to be there with him more than anything. "Is that better?" he smirked, showing off his well-defined chest.

"I think you should go a little lower," I whispered, biting my lip and stretching, trying to get a better glimpse on the screen.

"What have I turned you into?" he mused as his eyes

darkened and became more hooded.

"You know alcohol makes me bolder."

He chuckled, shaking his head at me. "Yes, I've noticed that. How did your evening go?"

"Boring," I sighed. "I miss you."

"I miss you too, Baby." I loved it when he called me *Baby*. "As soon as I'm free, I'll fly you over to me." I nodded, watching his eyes start to glimmer with playfulness. "But right now, if you are feeling *bold*, why don't you pleasure yourself while I watch?" *Oh, he doesn't think I'll do it! Ha.*

"You don't think I will?" I questioned. "I did last time."

"You did, but I wasn't *watching* you last time."

"So...I run my hands down my body, imagining my hands are yours. Is that right?" I asked with a soft groan, slowly caressing my breasts.

"Holy fuck, Jade!" Oliver almost dropped his phone as he watched me. After a moment, I angled my phone, placing it on the bedside table so he could see all of me. "You're really...oh, fucking hell...you are! Fuck, Jade, I wish I was there with you right now."

"You need to tell me what to do. What would you do to me right now if you were here with me?"

"Pull those hard nipples, Beautiful. Keep teasing yourself but imagine your fingers are mine. You know how much I love pleasuring you with my fingers." I did as Oliver asked, moaning as I closed my eyes and became lost in the sensation. "Shit, Jade. The things I could do to you if I was there."

"Like what?" I yearned, stroking over my clit. Shit, I was so wet already.

"You really want to know?"

"Ugh...yes," I begged, needing to hear his voice to bring me to my climax. I was so close already and I hadn't really done anything—how was that even possible?

"I'd be eating you out right now, if I were there...shoving my tongue so far inside your pussy, you'd be seeing stars."

"Yes," I moaned, struggling with the pleasure burning inside me as I set a frantic pace with my fingers. Shit, Oliver said pussy. He was driving me to the edge with just his words.

"Holy shit, Jade, you look so fucking sexy. That's it, Beautiful...let go for me, I need to see you cum." I fell at that moment, drowning in his command. When I finally gazed up at the phone screen, he was still watching me with hooded eyes. "Do you feel better for that?" he smirked.

"Yes, but I can't wait until you can take over."

"Me, either, Beautiful. Me, either," he sighed deeply. "I should probably let you sleep now, though. When are you flying back home?"

"Tomorrow morning," I yawned, glancing over at the clock on the nightstand. It was almost one o'clock in the morning. Damn, where had the time gone? "Don't I get to see you climax?" I pouted.

"Not tonight. I want to be inside you the next time I cum."

"Oh!" I gasped. "Now you're making me horny again."

"Call me when you get back tomorrow. I'm going to try and wrap things up here as quickly as I can."

"You mean I might get to see you soon?" I beamed.

"Yes," he grinned. "Sweet dreams, Beautiful, and remember to take some painkillers for your headache in the morning."

"I'm not *that* drunk, but goodnight," I giggled.

"Goodnight." He was chuckling as we disconnected our call, and it was only a matter of seconds before he had sent me a text message.

You are so fucking sexy! I'll be dreaming of eating out your sweet pussy tonight. ;) Night xxx

I was tempted to play along with his little game, but I wasn't sure how shy Jade would react to Oliver's dirty mouth, so I settled for a simple reply.

I can't wait. Make sure it's very soon. ;) Night xxx

* * *

"Why the hell do you have a big goofy grin on your face this morning?"
Drew asked as we ate breakfast in my bedroom. He had just gotten rid of his target, minus her keycard. We'd already met our contact and handed over the cards earlier, so our mission was complete.

"Maybe because I got a good night's sleep last night, unlike some," I teased, biting into my toast.

"I was on a job."

"You didn't need to sleep with her, Drew," I pointed out. "You could have easily taken her keycard while you had your tongue down her throat at the bar."

"But then my dick wouldn't be as happy as he is this morning."

"You are such a *guy*!" I laughed, shaking my head.

"Come on, Jelly Bean, eat up. We need to leave to catch

our flight in half an hour. Then you can tell me what has you grinning so much this morning." Childishly, I stuck my tongue out at him. There was no way I would be telling Drew about my call with Oliver. It didn't matter how much he bugged me on the flight back home—my lips would be tightly sealed.

* * *

I was unpacking after my trip to Miami when my phone rang. When I looked at the caller ID, I automatically smiled. It was Oliver. Blushing from head to toe, I thought back to our FaceTime call last night.

"Hey," I answered. "I was just about to call you. I just got home."

"Have you unpacked yet?"

"I was just about to," I replied.

"I'm heading to Macon now. I can pick you up in the jet at Clearwater airport in a few hours."

"Are you trying to show off with a private jet, Oliver?" I teased, feeling my heart deflate. This was it—my last weekend with him.

"It's the quickest way I get to see you."

"I can understand that. Where do I go when I get to the airport?"

"I'll meet you outside the VIP lounge."

"Okay," I breathed, trying to calm my racing heart, "I'll be there."

"Are you sure? I know I've dropped this on you at the last minute, but I remembered you saying you were free for the week once you got back from Miami. That gives us what—four days together if I need to get you back home by Monday morning?”

“It’s fine. I don’t even have to really pack, either. I’ll just need to add a few clean clothes.”

“Oh, you won’t need *that* many clothes.” His tone was pure sex and I knew exactly what he was thinking. I had to hold my legs together as thoughts of what he would do to me flashed through my mind. *This man could affect me over the phone in casual conversation. Um...wow!*

“Oliver, I’m meeting your family. I’ll need nice clothes.”

“Oh, my father is in hospital right now, but he’ll hopefully be out by the weekend. I thought we could go get him together.”

“That’s fine with me,” I muttered, swallowing hard. Could I really do this—play *happy family* with Oliver while stealing from his hard drive behind his back? His father had Alzheimer’s for Christ’s sake. *Jade, you have to; you have no choice.*

“Call me when you get to the airport. I’ll come and meet you after you’ve been through security.”

“Okay.”

“I can’t wait to see you, Jade. I’ve missed you so much.” It had only been just over two weeks since we’d seen each other, but deep down, I felt the same way.

“I’ve missed you, too,” I muttered, wiping my eyes before the tears began to form. I needed to get my shit together and soon.

“See you in a few hours, Beautiful.” After our goodbyes we both hung up.

Immediately, I called Sonia to let her know I was heading to Macon. She was pleased and wanted the mission closed up as quickly as possible.

In order to gain access to Oliver's files and download the one I needed, I'd been given a new decoder from Intelligence when I stopped by a few weeks ago. They also gave me a new GPS tracker for my cell phone.

I tried to call Drew next, knowing that he'd gone out to get us some lunch. He was going to stay at my apartment for a bit of downtime until he was assigned to his new target. Drew hated spending too much time at headquarters, just like I did.

He walked through the door just as I was dialing his number. "There's been a change of plan," I announced, moving to help him with the groceries. "Jeez, Drew, how much food did you buy?"

"I'm hungry. What's the new plan, then?" he asked, placing the bags down on my counter.

"I'm going to Macon."

"He called? Wait—is he the reason for your goofy grin? Did you know you might be seeing him?" Damn, he was asking way too many questions.

"No. He managed to get some free time, so he just sprung this on me five minutes ago."

"When are you going?"

"Right now. I'm meeting him at the airport in a few hours," I stressed, rushing around quickly.

"Jade, breathe. It's going to be fine. Why don't you go have a shower and get yourself ready, and I can drop you off at the airport when you're done."

"I'm not sure I'm ready for this," I whimpered.

"Of course you are. I've just watched you charm the pants off a guy in Miami. You stole his access card without even having to take him to bed. You're amazing."

"You could have done that with your target, too," I pointed out, crossing my arms.

"I know, but I was horny," he snorted, "and I knew *you* wouldn't give me any."

"Eww! You know I don't see us that way. It would feel like incest. Shit! You *were* joking about that orgy with Georgie and me last week, weren't you? Drew, I think of you as a brother."

"I was joking, Jelly Bean. I see you as a sister, too. Now go and get ready," he ordered with a stern look.

* * *

Two hours later, I was heading to the airport in Drew's SUV.

"Have you got everything? The decoder, your passport, your..."

"Yes, Drew," I laughed, interrupting him while pulling my phone out to call Oliver.

He answered on the second ring. "Are you almost here? I'm waiting outside departures. I wasn't sure you'd know how to get to the VIP area."

"You can't wait any longer to see me, can you?"

"You know me too well," he chuckled.

"I'm about five minutes away. I'll see you *very* soon."

"I'll be waiting," Oliver breathed before we both hung up.

"Damn, Jelly Bean. I've never seen you *that* smiley on the phone before. He *was* the reason for your goofy grin this morning, wasn't he?" I didn't answer him. "Please promise me you won't do anything stupid."

"Like what?" I frowned.

"Like telling him the truth. That guy is in love with your *character,* not the real you. Just think about how he would feel if he knew the truth—if he knew this was all a lie conjured up just to steal from him. You can't go into fantasyland thinking this could ever work out." I knew Drew was right, but Oliver was unlike any lover I'd ever had. It was natural that I was going to miss him. I knew guys like him were a rare breed, and I didn't mean the money aspect of his life. "You'll find a guy when you're out of all this, Jade, and he'll give you what you need. Trust me." As Drew spoke, my eyes fell on Oliver as he waited outside the airport for me. In a crowd of people, he *still* stood out to me. How could Drew think I'd ever find another man like him? Oliver was dressed in a well-tailored black suit with a white shirt and pale blue tie. Damn, he looked delicious!

"There he is," I gasped at Drew. "You can pull over anywhere here."

"Is that him in the suit?" he muttered as Oliver noticed us in the SUV. His face looked troubled for a few short moments before he quickly pulled himself together. *Oh, was someone jealous of Drew?*

"Yeah," I replied, smiling and waving at Oliver.

"Damn, he looks seriously rich. Look at all those men behind him. Molly said he was a hunk, but even *I* have to admit he's a hottie." This conversation was turning a little strange. Drew crushing on Oliver, too—that was just wrong.

"You're a *married* friend of mine, okay?" I quickly stated once the car came to a stop.

"*Married?* Oh, come on!" Drew complained.

"Please? For me?" I begged, moving to open the door. I needed to feel Oliver's touch and I couldn't wait a moment longer. Drew nodded, so I flew out of the SUV into Oliver's waiting arms.

Our lips crashed together instantly, and his cool, fresh scent washed over me as our tongues danced slowly together. I could feel his hands snake down my body, finding a place on my hips as the kiss continued. My own hands were wrapped tightly around his neck. Christ, I couldn't get enough.

"Don't mind the rest of us," Drew coughed minutes later. *Damn you, Drew! I haven't had my fill yet.*

"Hi," I giggled at Oliver once we broke apart.

"Hi," he grinned, a little dazed as he ran his fingers through my hair.

"Oh, this is Drew. He's the husband of one of my good friends."

"Nice to meet you, Drew," Oliver smiled, shaking his hand while looking a little relieved by my comment. His men were quick to take my bags that Drew had left on the sidewalk.

"You, too. I'll see you soon, *Jelly Bean*," Drew winked, getting back into his SUV.

"Jelly Bean?" Oliver frowned at me.

"Don't ask," I sniggered. "I have no idea *where* that name came from."

"Hmm..." Oliver mused, pulling me back into his arms. "I'm not sure I like that he has a nickname for you and I don't."

"You do have a nickname for me," I pointed out, running my hands down his chest.

"I do?"

"Beautiful?"

Oliver grinned, leaning down to kiss my lips softly. "That's just a true statement," he whispered against my lips. "*You,* Jade

Gibbs, are the most beautiful woman I have ever seen."

"Stop trying to make me blush." I hit his chest and then looked away from him, avoiding eye contact.

"Come on, let's get you to the jet," he winked, letting his men lead the way with my bags.

I practically flew through security. It seemed that when you were with a multi-billionaire, you didn't have to wait in any lines.

When Oliver escorted me onto the tarmac and I saw the private jet, my mouth dropped open a little.

"It's just a plane, Jade," he muttered into my ear.

"But it's *your* plane."

"This is nothing—wait until you see the mansion back home." Oliver pulled me along with him, allowing me to step into the aircraft first.

It was absolutely stunning inside, with six plush, white leather seats and a huge plasma TV screen. I could also see a cabinet for drinks set in black marble with a gold trim around the corners.

"This jet doesn't come with a bedroom, unfortunately," Oliver whispered into the crook of my neck. "If I'd bought this after I met you, I would have insisted on one."

"You mean I don't get to join the mile high club?" I pouted.

"Jade, the flight is only an hour and I have a few business calls to make, but I promise if you want to join *that* club, we can do it another time." He winked with a smirk to emphasize his statement.

Once we were onboard, we took our seats and buckled in quickly. After the plane was up in the air, the stewardess came and offered us some refreshments.

Oliver had a light beer while I decided to have a small glass of white wine.

"Wine?" he questioned, pulling his laptop out of the bag at his feet.

"I thought I'd act a little sophisticated for once. After all, I *am* meeting your family this weekend."

"You're fine just the way you are." Oliver was thoughtful for a moment as he watched me.

"So, who do I have the pleasure of meeting this weekend?"

"Well, there is my uncle, Richard, who you already know. Then there is his wife, Claire—she is a sweetheart—and my twin cousins, Tom and Sam." That was it? "Tom and Sam might not be home until the weekend, though. They're away at college at the moment."

"Which university?" I asked in interest.

"They're both at Harvard," he chuckled. "Richard wanted them to go to Yale because that's the traditional 'Kirkham' education. I'm glad the boys got their own way."

"Did you go to Yale?"

"Yes. I would never have gone against *my* father." I could see admiration in his eyes as he spoke. It was clear he still idolized his dad.

"Hmm... Let me try to guess what you studied," I mused, tapping my chin. Oliver was hanging on my every word as his eyes were slowly exploring each inch of my body. I crossed my legs, knowing it would give him more of a view of thighs. The pale pink cotton dress I was wearing was quite short anyway. "Was it business by any chance?"

"Jade, how on earth did you guess that?" he gasped, pretending to be shocked.

"I'm just that clever."

"That you are." Oliver's phone rang just as he was about to continue. "Sorry, Jade. Please excuse me for a moment." I nodded, gazing out the window and watching as the plane broke through the clouds. I loved flying—just taking in the world below me. It gave me a real sense of freedom to be so far up in the sky. "Yes, Abigail." Oliver listened for a few moments before responding. "I'm not interested in a meeting. I've already informed N.A.T.O. You can tell Miss Windom that I will not be doing business with her." Oliver's tone was harsh and angry. "I really don't care *what* she says. It's all a load of bullshit, anyway. They are *my* machines, and I will not be branching out with *any* other companies." Jesus, he even looked sexy when he was shouting. "If she has a problem with that, tell her to arrange a meeting with me and I will tell her face-to-face next week!" With that, Oliver hung up. "Sorry about that," he stressed, running his hands through his hair. He was really worked up.

"Problems running your empire?" I murmured, standing up and moving his laptop before sliding onto his lap. His arms automatically wrapped around me.

"It's nothing I can't handle." His hands began to stroke down my leg. "Are you trying to distract me?"

"I only came over for a kiss," I smirked, leaning down and pushing him against his seat as my lips locked with his.

"You have a very calming effect on me," Oliver muttered against my lips, causing my stomach to flutter at his words. I was glad I could relax him.

CHAPTER FOURTEEN

The rest of the flight was relaxing. Oliver had to make a few phone calls like he mentioned earlier, so I gazed out the window and got lost in my own thoughts as we flew closer to his family home.

As soon as the plane touched down, butterflies began to fill my stomach. I'd done countless missions in the past, so why did ending this one feel so different?

"Remember what I said about my apartment in New York?" Oliver muttered into my ear as the limo pulled onto a side road. I nodded, frowning slightly. "The same goes for this mansion. Try to remember that I was *born* into this. It's not who I am. I don't want to scare you off with my wealth." Just as Oliver finished speaking, my eyes fell on the mansion.

Holy shit! It was huge. The building was set in gray granite, with two tall pillars at the front entrance. I had to stop counting the large bay windows after number fifteen because there were just too many. It was the kind of mansion you'd imagine royalty to have, and it took my breath away.

"*This* is your family home?" I managed to ask after a few moments.

"Yep." Oliver looked at me coyly. "Do you want to take a look around? My family will be on the west side of the building,

I expect."

"Are you going to give me the grand tour?"

"Of course," he grinned, taking my hand and leading me inside.

Oliver showed me room after room, making my head spin with all the information he was giving me—from stories about the antiques, to how many features in the mansion were originals. All that was running around my head as he spoke was: 'This guy is so rich—stupidly rich.'

"This is my office," he muttered, touching my shoulder and pulling my attention away from what I believed was an original *Van Gogh.* "Jade, are you okay?"

"Is that a Van Gogh?"

"Yes, my great grandfather purchased it."

"This place is amazing, Oliver."

"You've only seen half of it so far," he chuckled, opening his office by entering a code into the security panel on the wall. *Using the year you were born as the passcode?* Oh, Oliver, why are you making this all too easy? "There isn't much in here, really. This used to be my father's office." He seemed lost in a memory as he spoke. "I used to love this room as a child. I would sit in his chair and pretend to be him." As I looked around, my eyes fell on his computer on the desk; that had to be the hard drive I was looking for. The office itself was very dated and full of dark wood, but it had more of a rustic feel to it than anything. "Can you see what I meant about the desk?" Oliver's voice was husky in my ear. "I could lay you over this one so much better than the one in New York."

"Oliver, you said this used to be your father's office. We can't do *that* here."

"We could…" I felt his fingers trace down the side of my body and stop near the bottom of my skirt.

"I thought I was meeting your family," I replied, slapping his hand away playfully.

"Fine. We'll go find Richard and Claire, and *then* I'll show you the master bedroom," he winked, taking my hand again.

We found his aunt and uncle in the grand kitchen a few minutes later. Claire was exactly as I had expected—tall and elegant, with long brown hair and a caring smile.

"It's wonderful to finally meet you, Jade," she beamed, pulling me into a tight hug. "How are you finding the house? Not too daunting I hope?"

"It's a beautiful place," I smiled, looking toward Oliver, who was glaring at his uncle for some reason.

"We thought we'd eat in here tonight. The boys won't be back until Saturday, so there is no point in using the dining room." Claire looked at Oliver.

"That's a good idea," he replied, pulling me tight against his side. "I was just going to show Jade the outside and then the master suite upstairs."

"Don't let us keep you. We can have a proper conversation at dinner," Claire beamed.

"It's lovely to see you again, Jade," Richard replied before Oliver led me out.

"What was *that* about?" I questioned as we ascended the grand staircase. He'd skipped showing me the gardens. I had the feeling he was keen to get me upstairs.

"What was that about?"

"You and your uncle," I continued.

"You noticed that?" Oliver shook his head at me. "You're

an observant little thing, aren't you?" He had no idea.

"I hope I haven't…"

"Jade, it wasn't about you," Oliver soothed, pulling me into his arms. "My uncle and I clash a lot when it comes to running the business. Don't worry about it." I couldn't help but worry. Did Richard suspect me for some reason? Was he going to be keeping a close eye on me while I was here? That would make my mission a lot more complicated. I'd have to see how the next few days went before I tried to get into Oliver's office.

"Here we are," he announced, pushing the double doors to the master suite open.

"Jesus!" I gasped, walking in and noticing that our belongings had already been dropped off. The room was as big as Oliver's bedroom in New York. It was an old style room, set in gold, light wood and fine dark fabrics. "What is it with you and huge bedrooms?"

"I don't care about the size of the rooms. It's the memories made in them that count," he mused, wrapping his arms around my waist. "How about we make some memories right now?" Oliver started undoing my dress before he'd even finished speaking.

Knowing how little time we had left together, I couldn't resist.

* * *

"Are you sure I look okay?" I asked, checking myself in the mirror again.

"It's only dinner in the kitchen, Jade," Oliver chuckled. My eyes fell on his naked body as he began to get dressed in faded blue jeans and a gray T-shirt.

"I know, but I want to make a good impression. Maybe I'll go for the pink dress," I mused, looking back to the mirror and tilting my head.

"You look amazing." Oliver was suddenly behind me, his lips grazing down my neck. It had been a wonderful, lazy afternoon. We hadn't moved from the large four-poster bed in hours, but were too lost in each other to really care. He was intent on making as many *memories* as we could before dinner.

"Does your uncle like me?" I asked, looking at him in the mirror behind me.

"Why do you ask?"

"I don't know...I just..." I let my eyes fall from his, unable to finish my sentence. Oliver turned me around to face him, then brought his hand under my chin so I would look up at him.

"It's me, Jade, not you. My uncle is skeptical about anyone I date. It's worse this time, though, because he knows how I feel about you."

"How do you feel about me?" I whispered. I had no idea why the question fell from my mouth, but once it did, I hung on his every word.

"You haven't worked that out yet?" Oliver's eyes were soft as he cupped my face. "You must know that I've fallen for you, Jade." I didn't even realize tears were trickling down my face until he wiped them away with his thumb. "Hey, it's okay," he soothed. "I know all of this is a lot to take in. I'm not trying to rush you or push you into anything, but you have to know that no woman has ever made me feel the way you do. When I touch you, I feel as if I'm on fire. You make me come alive. I'm not just some rich, multi-billionaire boss anymore—I'm just me, and I can't thank you enough for making me feel that way."

"Oliver," I whispered as the tears began to fall thick and fast.

"Sweetheart, what's wrong?"

"I'm not the kind of girl you should put your trust in," I sobbed. "I'll end up breaking your heart." I was completely losing it. *What the hell was wrong with me?*

"Now that's not true. You can open up to me, Beautiful. Please tell me why you're crying?"

"I...I...I'm not a good person, Oliver." I pushed away from him. "You can't have feelings for me—you just *can't*!"

"It's a little too late for that now." When his troubled eyes met with mine, I tried to look away, but the force of his gaze had me immobilized. I knew that look; I'd seen it before. It was the look of a man in love. *Shit! Shit! Shit!*

It wasn't the real me Oliver had fallen for, though. Shy, insecure Jade had played her part well, and Oliver had fallen right into her trap. "You have to see what we could have, Jade. You told me you weren't going to hold back anymore. Open up to me, please? Tell me how you feel."

"That was under different circumstances," I whimpered, trying to stop my sobs.

"What are you so afraid of?" He placed his hands on either side of my face and stared into my eyes. "I'll never hurt you, Jade. You're safe with me, I promise." I believed every word he was saying. Oliver wouldn't hurt me, but I would *destroy* him.

I couldn't let this go any further, for either of our sakes; it *had* to end this weekend.

"Can we talk about this later? I'm already going to have puffy eyes when we go down to dinner with your aunt and uncle." Oliver sighed heavily but nodded, finally letting me go. I was quick to excuse myself, heading into the bathroom to splash some cold water on my face. *Jade Phillips crying? Why couldn't I control my damn emotions?*

Oliver sat on the edge of the bed, watching me touch up my makeup in the mirror.

"What are you thinking?" I asked when a frown marred his handsome features.

"I just realized that I hardly know anything about you. Your job and love of *The Killers* is pretty much the extent of it."

"There isn't much to tell." I turned toward him, smiling weakly.

"What about your family?" I froze on the spot with my lipgloss pressed to my lips. My family wasn't something I *ever* thought about anymore, and the reminder hurt. They were part of the past—not that it mattered. When you became a Seductor you had to leave everything behind, and leaving my family was the easiest part for me after what happened to my sister.

"I don't speak to them anymore," I stated calmly.

"You don't speak to *any* of your family?" he gasped. "And you're only telling me this now?"

"It isn't a big deal, Oliver. You don't know anything about it. Please, can we change the subject?" I pleaded.

"I wish you'd open up to me."

"You can't just throw all of this at me and expect me to accept it. You know all *this* isn't really me." I waved my arms around, trying to accentuate the bedroom I was standing in.

"I've always made it clear about my wealth. I told you to ignore it. I was born with it, but it doesn't define me."

"You say that, but could you really live without it?" I asked, turning to join him on the edge of the bed.

"Yes," Oliver murmured. "I could live without it. My line of work isn't easy, Jade. I have tough decisions that I make on a daily basis. All I'm asking for is to have someone to come home to—someone to build a life with. I thought that was what you wanted. I mean, why else…"

"Oliver," I placed my fingertips to his lips, "we don't have to do this now. We have all weekend." With what I hoped was a reassuring smile, I kissed him.

"I'm sorry," he breathed against my lips. "I really don't mean to be overbearing."

"Let's just go and have dinner with your family," I suggested. A bit of distance from him at the dinner table was just what I needed right now.

* * *

"Richard tells me you're in the interior design business," Claire smiled, refilling my wine glass. Dinner had been amazing, and we were now sitting in a comfortable lounge on large, lavish black couches.

"Yes, I deal mainly in artwork," I replied.

"That must take you around the world."

"It does. I'm very lucky. I've been admiring all the pieces you have here. The Van Gogh is amazing." As a Seductor, you were taught to steer the conversation, making sure to never give too much away.

"Oh, yes! I've been trying to get Richard to put it up for auction for a while now, but he won't," Claire grumbled, looking over at her husband.

"It's priceless, Darling," he replied. "We're not selling it."

"Doesn't Oliver get a say in this?" she pouted.

Oliver held his hands up and laughed. "I've already told you—I'm staying out of this one."

"That seems like a wise choice," I grinned at him.

"Are you sure you don't want us to get your father on Sunday?" Richard turned to Oliver. "It wouldn't be a problem. You don't know what state of mind he'll be in." Oliver was thoughtful for a moment, looking out into space.

"Perhaps you're right," he finally said. "You really don't mind?"

"Once he's settled back in, we'll come and get you and Jade," he offered. Oliver nodded, sipping his beer.

If Richard and Claire were heading out on Sunday, that would be the best time to try and get into Oliver's office. I'd have to wear Oliver out first and wait until he was asleep, but it was the best plan I had so far.

"Your aunt and uncle are lovely," I sighed, slipping into bed later that night.

"Thank you." I watched Oliver strip to his boxers before sliding in next to me. I was only wearing a black silk nightie. "They seem quite taken with you."

"Even your uncle?" I giggled, feeling his hands glide underneath my nightie.

"We'll work on him," he whispered, pulling the silk from my body. "Why did you even bother to put that on?"

"Maybe I like it when you take my clothes off," I winked.

"Mm…you do have a point," he snarled, leaning down and pulling on my left nipple with his teeth. I arched up to him, my fingers finding a home in his hair.

His hands began to wander my body, leaving a fiery trail wherever they touched. I'd never burned so much for a man before.

"I need you, Jade." The desperation in his voice was clear; Oliver wasn't just talking about tonight. I answered him with an urgent kiss, knowing I couldn't be truthful. Touch was all I had to show him what he meant to me.

His lips began to travel down my torso, not breaking away for even a moment. How many times had Oliver gone down on me? I had no idea, but each time was more intense as he learned from my body. The feeling of his tongue as he licked across my clit was enough to make me bolt up from the bed. It was too much.

"I want you to ride me, Jade," Oliver cooed while he coaxed me down from my climax moments later. "I want to watch your body take pleasure from mine." That alone made me groan. "Can you do that for me?"

"Yes," I panted, feeling his fingers tease my entrance.

"Shit! You're so wet already. Are you that desperate for me?"

"Yes!" I groaned, moving to push him against the pillows. *Where was shy Jade?*

"That's it, Beautiful," he encouraged. "Just feel the desire and go with it."

I straddled his lap, closing my eyes as I felt his hands grope my breasts. When he began to twist both nipples, I rubbed my heated sex over his erection.

"Oh, ugh...yes," he muttered. What I would give to let go and really fuck this guy. I couldn't afford to do that, though—not now that I was so close to the end of the mission.

"Am I doing this right?" I asked, biting my lip and rocking my hips.

"You're teasing me is what you're doing," Oliver snarled. "Take me in, Beautiful. All of me." I did as he asked, bracing myself by gripping his shoulders as I slid his length deep inside me. "Oh...yes...that's it. You feel so good!" I threw my head back, losing myself in the feeling of being so full.

Oliver began to rock beneath me, lifting my hips up and down.

"I thought I was supposed to be riding you? You're doing all the work," I gasped as he began to bounce me faster up and down his member.

"You can fuck me slowly after this. I need to watch you come undone above me."

With that, he continued his attack, slamming me up and down while his lips devoured my breasts. I was scratching at his chest, trying to find some sort of control, but I was already losing it. Each time Oliver slammed me down onto his length a shot of euphoria hit me, and it just kept building and building.

"Can you feel that?" he murmured.

"Y...ugh...yes!" I panted, feeling my orgasm start to rise to the surface.

"You might not be able to tell me with words how you feel, but your body is another matter."

"O...Oli...Oliver!" He was leaving me hovering just out of reach of my climax. It was infuriating, but it also felt so good.

"What can you feel, Jade?"

"Y...you!"

"You can do better than that," he teased, slamming me

down hard on his length again. I was going to lose my shit at any moment.

"D...desire!" I cried out. "I can feel...how much my body wants you."

"Mm...that's better." He snaked his hand down the front of me while still bouncing me up and down. Sweat was starting to gather on my forehead, and when his fingers made contact with my clit, I exploded around him.

"Holy shit!" I screamed as I fell hard.

Oliver was gazing up at me when I finally opened my eyes.

"Are you ready to fuck me slowly now?" he smirked, cupping my ass. I could feel his length inside me, still rock hard and wanting more.

I smiled sexily and rolled my hips.

Oliver, I was born ready.

CHAPTER FIFTEEN

I was hardly ever sick, but Saturday morning I woke up with the worst stomach cramps I'd had in years. Of all the weekends it could happen, it just *had* to be this one.

I managed to make it into the bathroom without waking Oliver, but by the time I came back out, he was sitting on the edge of the bed waiting for me.

"Are you okay?" he asked in concern, standing up to greet me. I held my hands up to him as I felt the nausea suddenly wash over me again. Not wanting to get sick on him or his carpet, I rushed back into the bathroom. "Jade?" I could hear him calling me from outside the door, the worry evident in his voice. "Sweetheart, can I do anything?"

"Just give me a minute," I called, dabbing my face with water. Shit, I really felt like crap.

He was pacing the room when I finally came back out. "Are you okay?" he stressed, crossing the room to get to me.

"I'm not feeling too good, Oliver," I pouted. He pulled me into his arms, stroking my forehead softly.

"You do have a slight temperature," he muttered.

"I never get sick," I grumbled. "We could still try and go out for the day. I'm sure the fresh air will do me good."

"Oh no you won't!" Oliver scooped me up in his arms in one quick move. "The only place you're going is back to bed."

"Put me down," I giggled, kicking playfully.

"I'll have to wait on you hand and foot."

"No, you won't," I protested as he placed me back in bed.

"Don't try and argue with me, Jade. You won't win."

"But you'll be bored if you're stuck here with me all day."

"If you weren't *sick*, I'd say spending the whole day in a bedroom with you was paradise," Oliver winked, caressing my face. "Now, you rest while I go and get you some water. Are you hungry at all?" I shook my head, my stomach rolling at just the *thought* of eating. "Okay, just water to start with, then."

"Thank you," I called when he reached the door. "I can't remember the last time someone looked after me when I was sick."

"You know there is nowhere else I'd rather be," he muttered, watching me lovingly. "Rest now. I'll be back with your water soon."

I must have dozed off because I woke up groggy with cool hands caressing my forehead.

"Hey sleeping beauty," Oliver beamed down at me. "You still have a temperature."

"How long have I been asleep?"

"A few hours. Here—sip some of this." Oliver helped me sit up before passing a glass of cool, refreshing water to me.

"Have you been here the entire time?"

"No. I had a few business calls to make, and I told my aunt and uncle that you weren't well. I couldn't resist teasing my aunt by saying it was her cooking."

"You didn't?" I gasped, horrified.

"Claire knew I was teasing—relax," Oliver snorted, lying back on the bed beside me.

"You're really just going to stay here while I'm sick?" I asked, completely shocked. This mansion was *huge* and there were probably a thousand things he could do while I was stuck in bed; he didn't need to stay here with me.

"Yes. Do you have a problem with that?"

"No," I smiled, leaning back against his chest. It was amazing how comforting it felt to be in his arms. The cramps in my stomach almost disappeared with his closeness.

"I could stay like this with you for hours. It's not just about the sex, Jade." I closed my eyes, trying to keep myself grounded. I couldn't get swept away with his words. "I want to know you, Jade—every little detail."

"You're not going to try and make me open up while I'm sick, are you?"

"Tell me at least one thing I don't know about you yet."

"I hate the smell of cabbage," I giggled into his chest.

"I guess that's a start, but you know that wasn't quite what I meant." I could hear Oliver's eyeroll in his voice.

"I'm quite a loner. Maybe that's why I enjoy my job so much." That was the truth; being a Seductor was all about independence. You couldn't rely on anyone.

"I guessed that about you when I first saw you in London."

"What were your first impressions of me?" I asked, rolling onto my stomach. I rested my chin on my hands and looked up at him.

"I'll answer that if you promise to tell me your first impressions of me, too."

"Deal," I grinned. This was going to be interesting.

"I spotted you the moment I walked into the bar." He did? I hadn't noticed that. "You had an air of confidence about you. It wasn't just your beauty that drew me in."

"What else was it?"

"I knew that confidence was a mask. The moment our eyes locked, I saw *inside* you. There is something deep inside you, Jade, and I desperately want to help you release it."

"I'm not hiding some huge secret, Oliver. Seriously, there is very little to tell you about me."

"You don't talk to your family. How can you say there is no huge secret?"

"Some families just don't get along. It happens," I shrugged, sitting up and trying to casually blow off the conversation. It seemed that Oliver had a different plan, though.

"Families don't just fall out, Jade. There is *always* a reason."

"Are you really going to try and push this when I'm not feeling well?" I fumed. "I don't really think that's fair, especially since I already told you I'm not ready to talk about it."

"I'm not pushing anything. I was just stating a fact." He was so damn confident, lying there with his arms behind his head. For once, I was happy Oliver was fully clothed in gray sweats and a white T shirt. I knew I'd end up throwing up today if I rode that magnificent cock of his.

"It sounds like you're pushing to me," I pouted, getting up from the bed.

"Jade, I'm sorry. I didn't mean it to come out that way. Please sit back down. You can tell me something else about yourself instead."

"No more questions about my family?" I confirmed, playing with my hands nervously. *Poor little Jade.*

"I promise. Come on, get back in bed before you catch a chill." Oliver pulled the comforter up for me, so I slid back into bed and right into his waiting arms.

"I've never finished a glass of water," I muttered into his chest.

"What?" he chuckled, sounding really confused.

"I always leave some water at the bottom of my glass. I have no idea why."

"That's...just weird, Jade."

"You said you wanted to get to know me," I giggled.

"I have all my books in alphabetical order back in New York. It relaxes me to know I can find a book easily."

"I think that's worse than leaving a glass of water," I snorted.

"I like to be organized."

"Yeah, I can just *imagine* the panic attack you'd have if you lost a copy of your 'How to Run a Weapons Company.' What would you do?"

"How did you know about that book?" Oliver pretended to gasp, playing along with my absurd joke.

"How else would a CEO run his company? I thought you all had training manuals."

"Trust me—sometimes I wish there *was* a manual."

"It must be incredibly stressful to have all that reasonability on your shoulders."

"It used to be," he whispered, pulling me closer to his chest. "But with you, I can finally put work to one side. Yes, I have a job, but I also have a life with you."

"A life?" I gasped, trying to keep the tremor out of my voice.

"Yes, a life," Oliver grinned, kissing my forehead. "Now you need to keep up *your* end of the deal." What the hell was he *talking* about? "You were going to tell me about your first impression of me?" *Oh yeah!*

"I thought you were a celebrity," I sniggered. "Everyone wanted to talk to you."

"You mean like a rockstar?" Oliver winked.

"I'm not even sure *rockstars* could wear a suit as well as you," I admitted.

"Now *that* is a compliment, especially since I know about the fetish you have for rockstars." Oh, he thought he was funny.

"Fetish?" I hit his chest playfully. "I like rock *music*, not rock*stars*."

"The singer is part of the package. Can we get back to your thoughts on me, now?"

"I wanted to jump your bones the moment I saw you at the bar," I blurted out.

"Really?" Oliver's eyes widened at my confession. "The moment you saw me?"

"Yes." I watched the smile on his face fade into a pout. "What is it?"

"We wasted dinner. I could have just taken you up to my bedroom the moment we met."

"You probably could have," I laughed.

"Mm...I could have had you what—another four times while we were eating dinner."

"Stop talking about sex when I'm sick," I pleaded.

"Sorry, Beautiful. How about I fix us something to eat, instead? Are you hungry?"

"I am, actually. Maybe something light like soup?"

"I'll see what I can rustle up." I had to giggle at him. Was he really going to cook? "Well, I'll see what the housekeeper has in the fridge."

"That might be best," I smirked, stretching. "I think I'll have a quick shower while I wait. It might make me feel better."

"Good idea. I won't be long." With that, he jumped off the bed and went in search of food.

The shower did wonders for my aches and pains, and I lost track of the time I'd been in there. It was only when I felt Oliver's naked body behind me that I snapped out of the daydream I was having.

"The food will be ready in an hour. Mrs. Pollen will bring it up for us."

"Then why are you in the shower?" I questioned, groaning as his hands began to massage my shoulders.

"I'm checking on you, of course," he purred into my ear, sending shivers down my spine.

"And you needed to get *into* the shower with me to do that, huh?"

"I needed to take a shower, too, and this way, we're conserving water."

I let out a loud laugh. Turning around, I wrapped my arms around his neck and drew him underneath the jets with me. "Do you energy save a lot?"

"How else do you think I became a multi-billionaire?"

"Wow! I never knew that was all you needed to do. I think I'll start being more energy conscious from now on." Oliver chuckled softly before stroking my wet hair. His hands continued down my back, pulling my body flush against his.

"We should wash quickly before I get carried away with

you and your sexy body."

"You came in and interrupted *me*. I'm already clean."

A gleam filled his eyes. "I could make you dirty again."

"No you won't! I'm sick," I warned.

"You better get your sexy butt out of this shower, then."

"You're throwing me out when I was here first?" I teased.

"No. I want you to stay, but I can't promise I'll be able to keep my hands off of you. You know how much I love it when you're *wet*." *Oh, Oliver.*

"Behave," I sniggered, trying to pull away from him. "If you want me to get out, then you need to let me go."

"I'm not sure I can," he muttered, backing me up so I was against the tiles. "Do you have any idea what you do to me?"

"I think I have an idea," I swallowed, feeling his erection pressed against my stomach.

"You *will* open up to me, won't you, Jade? Please tell me you want this as much as I do." Oliver's tone was dejected and it broke my heart. I knew I wasn't giving him any answers, but I refused to build his hopes up any more than I had to. There was a high probability that this would be the last weekend we ever spent together. *Stop thinking about that, Jade.*

"You really need to ask that?" I placed my hand on his face. "You can feel it in my body when you touch me. You *know* what you mean to me." Oliver crashed his lips against mine, taking my breath away.

I grabbed his slick, wet hair, tugging it as I let his kiss consume me.

"I'll stop with the heavy now," he winked as our lips finally broke apart. "Now get out of this shower before I molest you."

I got dressed quickly and had just finished blow drying

my hair when Oliver came out clean and dressed.

"You look much better," he commented, stroking my face as he walked past me.

"The shower did me good. I'm quite hungry now, too." Just as I spoke a knock sounded at the door.

"That will be the food." Oliver raced to the door and came back carrying a large silver tray.

"Mrs. Pollen's chicken soup is legendary. It will have you feeling better in no time."

"It smells amazing." I licked my lips, joining him at the small table by the window.

"She said the orange juice would be good for you, too. You need the vitamin C."

"How long has Mrs. Pollen worked here?"

"All my life. She's been here for over fifty years."

"Wow! *That* is a long time." I took a large sip of orange juice and nearly moaned. Damn, it was good.

"The estate isn't as hard to run as it used to be. We've shut a lot of it down," Oliver stated, watching me carefully. What was he thinking? "We only have Mrs. Pollen and Giles, the caretaker and butler, left working here."

"Is that because you're mostly in New York?"

"In some ways, yes." He took a deep breath before continuing. "My family is a lot smaller than it used to be. We don't need all this space now that Sam and Tom are away at school."

"What are they like—your cousins?"

"They're real jokesters." Oliver seemed lost in thought for a moment, laughing to himself. "But they are good boys. I'm hoping they'll decide to work for the company when they finish college."

"Will that lift some of the pressure off you?"

"I doubt it," he sighed. "But time will tell. Have you had enough soup?" he questioned when he noticed I'd finished my bowl.

"Yes, thank you."

We spent the rest of the afternoon watching old movies and talking about his childhood here in Macon.

Oliver certainly had a happier childhood than me, that was for sure, and I had to admit I was a little jealous.

***

When we finally made it downstairs, it was obvious by the noise that Oliver's twin cousins had arrived home.

"Tom, stop stuffing your face. Dinner will be ready in a few hours," I heard Claire scold before my eyes fell on the twin boys. *My, the Kirkham gene pool was strong.* They were good looking boys with light brown hair and deep blue eyes. They both looked as if they worked out, too.

"The wanderer returns. Oliver, I can't remember the last time I saw you here in Macon." One of the boys grinned, darting his eyes to me. "It's lovely to meet you, Jade. I'm Sam," he greeted, pulling my hand out and kissing my knuckles.

"That's enough of that, Samuel," Oliver teased, pulling Sam into a headlock and ruffling his hair. "Jade won't fall for your charms. You're *far* too young for her."

"What about me?" Tom smirked. "I'm older than him."

"Only by ten minutes—that doesn't count," Oliver replied breathlessly as Sam tried to struggle free.

"It's wonderful to meet you, Jade. Oliver hasn't shut up about you since you met," Tom snorted as Sam finally broke away from Oliver's grasp.

"So you two are identical twins?"

"Yep. We can wear our name badges this weekend, if you want," Tom winked.

"Don't fall for that, Jade," Oliver muttered in my ear, wrapping his arms around my waist. "They'll switch their badges just to mess with you."

"Hey, don't give our tricks away!" Tom glared.

"There is an easy way to tell them apart," Oliver continued, smirking at me.

"Are you going to tell Jade about the birthmark on my butt?" Sam blurted out. Tom burst out into a fit of laughter before Claire walked up behind them.

"You'll have to excuse my sons," she tutted.

"You get used to them," Oliver chuckled as Claire brought her hands up and smacked her boys in the back of their heads. Gazing at his family, I could see doing just that, and it made me realize just how lucky he was to have them.

CHAPTER SIXTEEN

Macon was a truly beautiful place. Oliver took me for a tour around his 'hometown' on Sunday when I was feeling better. Tom and Sam wanted to come with us, but Oliver managed to persuade them into believing that it wasn't a good idea. I had a feeling he didn't want to share me with his cousins.

He was a web of knowledge as we wandered around Macon, telling me all about the history of the town, as well as the famous faces that had been born here; they included Otis Redding, Little Richard, and Bill Berry, who I learned was the lead singer of REM.

His thoughtfulness continued as he took me to the Museum of Arts and Science. It was a perfect compromise—I had the art to look at while Oliver tried to explain some of the science to me.

"You're a great tour guide," I grinned as we were having lunch in the museum's restaurant.

"My father and I came to this museum almost every weekend. I used to hang on his every word."

"You're really close to him, aren't you?"

"Yes. Is it that obvious?" Oliver asked solemnly.

"Are you going to tell me what's wrong with him before

I meet him later?" I questioned. Richard and Claire would be bringing him home later this afternoon.

Oliver dropped his menu with a deep sigh, and I was hoping I hadn't upset him; this afternoon had been amazing— one I would treasure forever. "You're right. I *should* prepare you."

"If you don't want to talk about it…"

"No, it's fine. You could even Google it if you wanted to— my father's condition isn't a secret. I should probably be the one to tell you, though." I waited patiently for him to continue. "He has Alzheimer's, Jade."

It was times like these that I used to have to fake the waterworks, but just like *everything* with Oliver, the tears came naturally from the pain etched on his face.

"I'm so sorry," I whispered, stretching over the table to take his hand in mine.

"He hardly recognizes me anymore. He's been more confused than usual, which is why he was in the hospital. My uncle and I aren't sure how much longer we can keep him at the mansion with us. Even with the live-in nurse, it's becoming too dangerous. He needs *constant* supervision."

"Couldn't you bring in another nurse?"

"It has more to do with the mansion than anything. Richard wants to secure him in two rooms on the west side of the house, but I refuse to let my father be a prisoner in his own home," Oliver seethed, making me jump back at his sudden aggression. "Sorry," he winced. "It's not an easy subject for me. Parts of the house are triggers and they help him remember, so I don't want to take that away from him."

"You don't have to apologize," I soothed. "I can't even begin to imagine the strain you must be under."

"You have no idea how good it feels to have someone to talk to about this—other than my family." I smiled back as he squeezed my hand. I wanted to comfort him more, but giving him false hope felt wrong. "Was your last boyfriend this open with you?" *Whoa!* That was a sudden change of subject.

"Umm…no," I frowned, totally puzzled as to where Oliver was going with this.

"What was his name again?"

"Who?"

"Your last boyfriend." He really wanted to talk about *Mario*? Great, my favorite topic. Thank *Christ* I never actually dated him.

"Oh, Mario," I sighed, running my hands through my hair, doing my best to look uncomfortable.

"He was an idiot for cheating on you."

"I had a lucky escape. Mario wasn't the man for me," I stated, playing with my wine glass.

"And who is?" Oliver murmured, stretching out to take my hand.

"You already know the answer to that," I smiled shyly.

"Are you deliberately trying to avoid the question?"

"Maybe we should think about heading back after lunch, you know…since your father is coming home," I smirked. He nodded while grinning at me, completely unaware that I would probably be gone before his dad even made it home. Deep down, I wanted Oliver to be the man for me, but I had to remember it wasn't *me* he was falling for. This was all a charade.

When we arrived back at the mansion, I would need to put my plan to copy the hard drive in motion. I couldn't put it off any longer; it wasn't fair to either of us.

* * *

Oliver's aunt and uncle had already left by the time we got back.

"Mm...we have the mansion to ourselves. How about we make some memories in as many rooms as we can while we're alone?" he suggested, pulling me into his arms in the hallway outside the master suite.

"What about the staff and your cousins?" I giggled, feeling Oliver bite down on my neck.

"They're all getting my father's room ready."

"I think I'd feel more comfortable in the master suite." I gasped when Oliver's hands slipped into my panties while he stood behind me.

"Are you sure? We could start right up against this wall." Oliver slowly sunk two fingers inside me and I had to suppress a moan.

"Shit!" I braced myself on the wall as he pulled them almost all the way out before thrusting them in again. I needed to tire Oliver out so I could get inside his office, and letting him take me right here seemed like a good place to start.

"Do you like that? Anyone could find us here right now and see me playing with you." His words made even more moisture pool between my legs. "Mm...I think you like it, Jade." Oliver's other hand crept into my top, pulling the cups of my bra down. I had both hands on the wall as I got lost in the feeling of his fingers sliding in and out of my sex while his other hand massaged my breasts.

When I fell into the abyss, Oliver was quick to turn me

around and lift me up by my ass.

"That's enough of the exhibitionist, I think," he teased, crashing his lips against mine. "What am I turning you into?" I giggled against his mouth, wrapping my legs tighter against his hips as he started to walk.

As soon as my back hit the mattress, Oliver's hands were on me again, pulling at my dress. I sat up to make it easier for him, and the moment he pulled it over my head, I made quick work of the belt on his pants.

"You *are* becoming bolder, aren't you?" he chuckled as I gazed up at him, unbuttoning his jeans next.

Oh, to hell *with it.* I could be a little bolder now, right? I had wanted to go crazy on that amazing cock of his since the moment we met. This was my last chance, so why the hell should I hold back?

Licking my lips, I pulled his jeans and boxers down at the same time. His length sprang free, and my mouth began to water at the sight of him.

I took Oliver deep in my throat before he could even register what was going on.

"Whoa...fuck, Jade," Oliver grunted, trying to pull out of my mouth. His actions spurred me on, making me suck harder to hold him in place.

I grabbed his butt cheeks, drawing him in deeper. Relaxing my throat, I took in his full length and swallowed around him a few times before pulling back out, running my tongue along his entire member.

"Holy shit!" Oliver lost some of his control and grabbed my hair roughly. *That's right, Oliver, it's my turn now.* I grazed my teeth along his erection, swirling my tongue around the tip before taking him deep into the back of my throat again. I continued this for a few minutes before quickening my pace. Cupping his balls, I squeezed gently and felt him begin to twitch.

"Jade...oh, God, Beautiful...stop...I'm going...to..." I gazed up at Oliver, watching him come undone above me as he shot his hot liquid into the back of my throat. I swallowed everything he gave me without hesitation; it wasn't my favorite thing in the world, but the look of hunger in his eyes as he gazed down at me was worth it.

"I think you're right. You *are* making me a little bolder." I batted my eyelashes at him, wiping my mouth.

He growled low in his chest before quickly pressing me against the mattress and pouncing on me.

"Where the hell did that come from?" he groaned, sliding in between my legs.

"I was showing you the desire I have for you." I beamed up at him as he caressed my face.

"You're amazing, do you know that?" I wanted to believe his words, but Oliver wasn't falling for me. I was a Seductor. It was my job to make men fall in love with my character. However, this was the first time my heart had beaten frantically at my target's words.

"I'm nothing special," I giggled, pulling him down to my lips.

"You're wrong," he whispered. "You've bewitched me, Jade. So much so that I want you to move to New York and live with me. I've been thinking about it all day and I can't hold back anymore. I can't bear to be apart from you. I'm...in love with you, Jade. Please say you'll consider it."

My world shattered around his words. Oliver made it all

sound so perfect...so easy. I could even see it—Oliver and I living happily in New York—but it was a fantasy. If he knew the truth, if he knew who I really was, he wouldn't even want to touch me.

"Jade?" Oliver wiped my traitorous tears away as he watched me with troubled eyes. "What's wrong?"

"Nothing," I whimpered, pulling him back down to my lips. "Just love me, Oliver...please," I pleaded. He captured my lips and became lost in my body at the sound of my words.

Our lovemaking was relentless. Each time he thought we had finished, I would beg him for more. I knew he was getting tired as I rocked above him an hour later, pulling yet another orgasm to the surface, but I never faltered.

When we collapsed in each other's arms this time, I noticed he was drifting.

"I'll just go get us a drink," I whispered into his ear. Oliver hardly acknowledged me; he was already falling asleep.

With a heavy heart, I got changed and collected my small bag. I would be leaving my suitcase here. It would be impossible to make a quick escape while lugging that around with me.

I turned to look at Oliver one last time, sleeping peacefully in his bed, and then made my way downstairs.

The mansion was still quiet, but I was careful of my surroundings as I entered the passcode to his office and slipped inside.

His computer was quick to start up, which had my heart racing in my chest. A small part of me was praying the hard drive wasn't here, but this was the most obvious and most secure place for it to be. After all, Oliver only brought *trusted* people to his family home. My heart ached at the way I'd played him because he was a good man; he didn't deserve any of this. I couldn't think about how he would react when he woke up and found me gone, though. The man has just told me he loved me for Christ's sake. He was going to be broken in two.

I quickly typed in the password I'd learned from him in New York, but it didn't work. *Damn it!* The decoder would take a few minutes, and I didn't really have the time. Oliver could stir at any moment and come down to find me. Not to mention Tom and Sam were around the mansion somewhere.

I remembered Oliver telling me once that his password was the name and date of birth of a loved one and it made me think. Without really knowing why, I typed in my fake information. It was worth a try before I used the decoder.

Tears trickled down my face as all his files suddenly opened. *I was Oliver's password.*

I searched his files and gasped, quickly realizing that this *was* the hard drive I was looking for. *Everything* was here—even my background check. Oliver's uncle must have made him run one after we met in London.

The file name—S10301982—was staring right back at me, but my hands were frozen. I couldn't make myself move to copy the file.

Do it, Jade. You have no choice.

Without any more thought, I put the decoder into the USB port and pressed copy before quickly looking away. I couldn't watch the files being downloaded, knowing I was betraying Oliver.

These machines could kill millions of people, and I knew I should be worried. It wasn't in my job description to care, though. Doing so would cost not only my life, but Oliver's, as well. If *I* didn't steal these files, someone else would break into the house, steal the files, and kill the target. That was the protocol for any mission that had gone wrong. If a Seductor couldn't secure the steal, there was only one reason—the Seductor had become attached to their target. The contingency protocol was created to make sure no Seductor ever fell into that trap.

I had to do this...for Oliver. He may lose the plans to his top secret machine, but at least he would still have his life.

I glanced back at the computer screen after a few minutes, noticing that the files had been downloaded. After quickly turning everything off, I put the decoder and files into my bag.

My mission was complete.

As I wandered out of Oliver's office, the mansion was eerily silent. I looked up at the grand staircase, my body burning for one more glimpse of him. What good would that do, though?

I wasn't the girl for him. In time, I knew he'd forget me and meet someone new. I was tied to my job for another five years, and I couldn't picture a man like Oliver still being available after that long.

I should have just walked away—I knew that—but my feet had other plans and I began climbing the grand staircase before I even realized I had moved. *Jade, what are you doing? Oliver could be awake!* I didn't really care if he *was* awake; I needed to see him one more time. I would just have to disappear in the middle of the night if I got caught. I had the hard drive files now, so the worst part was over.

Slowly, I opened one of the double doors to the suite and peered around it. Oliver was still fast asleep, but he'd rolled over onto his side and was clutching a pillow.

I made my way to the side of the bed to gaze at him, trying

to memorize every detail of his pure perfection: from his well-defined, muscled chest, to the length of his eyelashes as he slept. Oliver was my dream man in every sense of the word.

I was thankful I'd been given this mission. Meeting Oliver Kirkham would always be *the* highlight of my life. It only saddened me that he would never know that.

I leaned down, pressing my lips softly to his forehead. "Thank you, Oliver," I whispered softly. "In another lifetime, I could have loved you and been very happy." He stirred slightly but didn't wake up.

Taking two steps back, I wiped my eyes as I watched him, then put my bag over my shoulder and walked away. Luckily, I left the mansion without anyone seeing me, and after waving down the first car that passed, I made my way to the airport.

I called Sonia and wired the files over to her while I waited for my flight back to headquarters. The *clean-up* for the mission was already in effect, which would make it impossible for Oliver to find me. The Seductors were all about protocol when a mission had been completed.

I should have been happy about that. Oliver might find out what I'd done in time and want to come after me, but he wouldn't find me.

I wasn't a fool, though. I knew what had happened to me over the last few months, and now that I was away from him, I could admit it to myself.

I'd fallen in love with Oliver Kirkham. He'd made me feel a desire like no other before, and having to give him up, well…it was like a part of me died when I walked away.

But, I was a Seductor. I couldn't sit around and mope all day about my lost love; I had just under five more years left on my contract before I was free. Who knew what would happen after that? Oliver might wait for me. A girl could dream, right?

For now, though, I had to move on and lock the memories of him away deep inside my heart.

As I glanced down at my iPhone, I sighed when I noticed that my mission status had already been updated at headquarters.

It was the closure I needed to begin to move on.

Target: OK2634—Oliver Kirkham
Seductor: 03JADE
Status: Mission complete.

ABOUT THE AUTHOR

B. L. Wilde

B.L. Wilde is a British author who has always loved the written word, and takes great pride in bringing her stories to life.

She lives in Worcestershire with her partner and their two spotty dogs.

B.L is a sucker for happy endings, but will always make her characters work for it.

If you enjoy romance, suspense and erotica, let your imagination run 'Wilde' with one of her books today.

PRAISE FOR AUTHOR

I am completely in awe of Ms Wilde's writing, it captivates me, makes me feel all these different emotions and it makes me want to read more and more.

> *- GOODREADS REVIEWER*

The moment I get the email from B.L. Wilde that says "are you up for reading a little something" I tend to do a little dance. The answer is always "YES!!!!" I absolutely adore the writing style and characters that Ms. Wilde gives us in every story.

> *- AUTHOR, ANDREA JOHHSON*

OMG OMG OMG , where to start ....I started reading this book at 11 am this morning and had read the full book 5 hours later, I never in my wildest dreams thought this book would grip me like it did. It had my bum perched firmly on the edge of my seat the whole way through.

> *- AMAZON REVIEW FOR DESIRE*

THE SEDUCTORS SERIES

Jade has worked as a Seductor in a secret organization for five years now. Her main job? To earn the trust of her targets and secure the object or information her company was hired to steal —by any means necessary. She's damn good at it, too. With five years left on her contract, she is handed an assignment that turns her world upside down. Oliver Kirkham is the attractive, young CEO of Kirkham Industries, a weapons manufacturing company, and is currently in possession of some very important blueprints—blueprints that could change the way war, as we know it, works. He's extremely focused and doesn't have time to date, at least until he comes to the rescue of a shy but very alluring Jade Gibbs. What happens when one night of passion turns into more? Will Jade allow her feelings for Oliver to get in the way of her mission? Or will she do what she was hired to do and secure the steal?

Hunger

Devotion

Clarity

Salvation

BOOKS BY THIS AUTHOR

Steel Roses Series

Natasha White has always been unlucky in love. The men she falls for only want one thing from her, and it isn't commitment. When her boss and on/off fling announces his engagement to another woman, she finds herself running from her feelings for him by taking a job as a personal assistant to the legendary rock god, Alex Harbour—half a world away. Her new boss is sexy, damaged, and insatiable, but Natasha has been a fan since she was a young girl. Conflicted by her emotions, she begins a love/hate relationship with the egotistical rock star. Alex's intentions toward her are clear from the moment they meet, but Natasha isn't about to run from one emotionless connection to another. She is determined to keep her distance from her childhood crush, by any means necessary. When lust begins to cloud her mind, however, she becomes hell bent on protecting her heart. What good could ever come out of falling for a rock star, anyway?

The Human Mating Site

Join Bella, a ray of pure sunshine and an avid steamy romance reader, while she searches for Mr. Right.

Mr. Wimp is the beginning of her story, as she splits from her husband. After twelve years together, Bella never thought she'd be back in the dating pool. She quickly realises how much of herself was lost in her relationship with her ex.

The human mating site isn't so bad, if all you want is some fun to gain your confidence back. Hell, Bella can even act out some of the scenes in the spicy romance books she has read! Online dating is full of amusing plot twists and sexy fun.

Bella soon learns that becoming single in your thirties has never been so sexually liberating.

The series will consist of 13 novellas, with 13 different Mr. Right Nows (that include plenty of grumpy, sexy, witty and alpha men), and will be released monthly.

Printed in Great Britain
by Amazon

35828757R00137